Required: one Doomsday weapon capable of ironing out the whole human race. It was a tall order, but then I thought I had a rather tall solution. Oddly enough, several of my junior scientists were quite enthusiastic about the project. They came up with such wild schemes as indestructable viruses, radio-activity saturation devices, even anti-gravity fields large enough to drain the planet of its atmosphere and so choke us all to death. I dismissed the more original and enthusiastic members of my team. Such people seemed to me to be rather dangerous.

Besides, by this time I had an idea of my own. It was elegantly simple . . .

Also by the same author, and available in Coronet Books:

Transit
All Fools' Day
The Venom Of Argus
The War Games Of Zelos
Death Worms Of Kratos
The Rings Of Tantalus
The Overman Culture
A Far Sunset
Seed Of Light
The Tenth Planet
Sea-Horse In The Sky
Kronk

Jupiter Laughs

and other stories

Edmund Cooper

CORONET BOOKS
Hodder and Stoughton

First published in Great Britain 1979 by
Hodder and Stoughton Limited

Coronet edition 1981

British Library C.I.P.

Cooper, Edmund, *b. 1926*
Jupiter laughs and other stories.
I. Title
823'. 9' 1FS PR6053.05469A15

ISBN 0-340-26462-4

The characters and situations in this book are entirely imaginary and bear no relation to any real person or actual happening

Printed and bound in Great Britain for Hodder and Stoughton Paperbacks, a division of Hodder and Stoughton Ltd., Mill Road, Dunton Green, Sevenoaks, Kent (Editorial Office: 47 Bedford Square, London, WC1 3DP) by Richard Clay (The Chaucer Press) Ltd., Bungay, Suffolk

This book is for my wife Valerie
who has shared so much, in so many
ways, of my writing life.

Introduction

SCIENCE FICTION IS a most peculiar literary genre. Many people seem to think that it is a product of our technological era; but it has a long and honourable tradition. Sir Thomas More's *Utopia* was a piece of science fiction which stimulated political and social development throughout Europe; Jonathan Swift's *Gulliver's Travels* was a strong piece of social criticism; Mary Shelley's *Frankenstein* posed the moral question of how far science should be allowed to go; Jules Verne optimistically dreamed of great scientific progress and wrote many entertaining novels on this theme; Samuel Butler's *Erewhon* questioned the social values of the Victorian age. The great giant, H. G. Wells, considered in his novels emotional, scientific and social problems. He also wrote most entertainingly of now conventional themes — space exploration and the invasion of Earth by aliens. Aldous Huxley's *Brave New World* was an indictment of the Pavlovian responses that could be generated to control people and social institutions. George Orwell's *1984* was a nightmarish vision of totalitarianism. And so on.

Nowadays most science fiction writers still seem to be concerned with space odysseys and scientific innovation. But there are some, notably Kurt Vonnegut and J. G. Ballard, who are more concerned with people than with gadgets.

In my early short stories I was fascinated by scientific and technological innovation. In my later short stories I became more concerned with moral issues — as, indeed, I have been in many of my science fiction novels. I was amazed to discover recently that two bibliographers — one in the north of England and the other in Australia — are trying to compile a complete list of my work. One of them recently sent me a working list, and I was also surprised to discover that I had written forty-two science fiction stories.

The first short science fiction story I ever wrote was *Falcon Chase*. It dealt with the visit to Earth of people from another world — a theme which has been dealt with by many other science fiction writers including the great H.G. In most of the stories I have read the visitors pose a threat to mankind. I chose to reverse the situation: mankind was a threat to them.

My next story was *The Brain Child* in which I chose to satirise our optimistic attitude to the development of computers. Both stories were written in the mid 1950s, which, in view of scientific, political and social change, now seems a very long time ago.

In 1954 the Astronomer Royal claimed that a man would never get out into space. At the time I was writing a story called *The Intruders,* which described the conditions on the surface of the moon. The story is overlong for the present collection, and I have excluded it, but it foretold with uncanny accuracy the conditions met with by Neil Armstrong when finally man set foot on the moon in July 1969.

My unhappy ability to prophesy was further developed in *Death Watch* — published in this collection — which told of the way American generals were trained to control a nuclear strike force. The story was written in 1960. Two years later I read an article in *Time* magazine which indicated that such training was in progress under the conditions I had described.

I have never regarded myself as a prophet, seeing it only as my duty to consider possible scenarios. Fortunately, most of the scenarios I consider have little chance of coming true.

But *The Life and Death of Plunky Goo*, written in the early 1960s, is uncomfortably close to the truth. The ruthless exploitation by advertising men of 'the child market' is becoming more and more vicious.

Another theme about which I felt very strongly was the development of microbiological weapons. It was this intensity of feeling that caused me to write the story *Judgment Day*. Unhappily, the major powers are still concerned with the prospects of microbiological warfare. One cannot help but feel that nuclear weapons are preferable.

I have been writing science fiction for over twenty years and have discovered that I am only at my best when I have a theme in which I deeply believe. The basic duty of a professional fiction writer is to entertain his readers and perhaps give them food for thought. I believe that I have a duty to myself and that is to put up for public examination ideas, themes and attitudes which have affected me deeply and personally. If I have succeeded in entertaining my readers while doing this, then I have succeeded in all I ever wish to achieve.

MADEHURST, SUSSEX
January 1979

Contents

Jupiter Laughs

THE TROOP OF horsemen moved slowly along the stony track through the desert. They were tired — all five of them — dead tired. They had done a lot of riding and a lot of killing. The killing had made them more tired than the riding. What kind of soldier could take any pleasure in killing kids that couldn't even walk, couldn't even sit up?

The sergeant sighed and glanced up at the night sky. Black, star-studded, peaceful. There was a big moon, too. It turned the desert into silver rocks and silver sand. The light was good enough to ride by, if you took it easy.

The sergeant looked back over his shoulder. That goddam star was still there. The bastard star that had caused all the trouble. But maybe there wouldn't have been any trouble if those three wise guys — bent fortune-tellers by the look of them — hadn't come to the city and stirred it up enough to get themselves admitted to the palace. Stupid bastards. Said they had been following the goddam star, said it was going to lead 'em to where a great king would be born. Stupid, stupid bastards!

Everyone knew the old king was nutty as a fruit cake. And mean. Real mean. Everyone knew it except those clever idiots with their fancy clothes and fancy ways. Maybe they thought they were on to a big con. Maybe they had been hoping to take the old devil for a hatful of gold. He was still cunning and vicious, but a bit simple-minded. Senile. It showed.

The star still looked as if it sat high over that god-forsaken town. Mercifully, the town was nearly a day's ride back there, hidden by the hills. The sergeant didn't want to see it, anyway. But he could still see it, in his mind's eye. And he could still hear it — the screaming; the shouting; the women offering themselves, anything, for the sake of their kids; their crazy menfolk trying to fight disciplined soldiers with hammers, knives, sickles, pieces of wood, bare hands.

But the king's soldiers did their thing, did what they were told to do. They slaughtered the kids — just like they were young suckling-pigs, which most of 'em were — chopped down enough of the men to discourage the rest, and had some of the women. They didn't have too many of the women. How the hell do you work up a woman when her old man has been knocked on the head and her kid's lying in its blood? But blood lust does funny things to men and women. The sergeant had heard that one poor bitch got herself screwed to death by a score of brawny heroes. They said that she was laughing herself silly and coming all the time.

Again, the sergeant sighed. It was going to take a lot of booze to wipe the memory of that night's doing. He shivered. Goddamit to hell, there wasn't that much booze in the world.

He noticed that someone had just come up by his side. The sergeant knew who it was without looking. The boy who used to be a shepherd. The bumpkin. But now he has whiskers and muscles hardened by a desert childhood. So now he was a man. And now he was a soldier. How old was he — sixteen, seventeen?

"Hey, Sarge. You think Herod's crazy? Some of the men are saying that he's flipped."

"Yes, he's crazy. We're all crazy. We live in a crazy world. You take his salt-money like I do. We do what he tells us. Now, who is more crazy, boy, him or us?"

The bumpkin scratched his head nervously. "I hadn't thought of it like that . . . But chopping all those babies, that was like, like a nightmare."

"You didn't have to be a soldier, son."

"What else was there for me?"

"You could have stayed with the sheep."

"What kind of a life is that, Sarge?" The bumpkin sounded hurt.

"What kind of a life is this, stupid? Did you have any of the women back there?"

"No, Sarge. It — it didn't seem right . . . I mean all that killing and all."

"There is hope for you yet," said the sergeant with a thin smile. "Now shut up and piss off."

Just as the bumpkin was dropping back, the sergeant said, "Mind you, Herod is really twisted. I know. I served him a long time. When he came to power, he butchered half the Sanhedrin, and then he started on the priests. After that, he chopped his wife, Mirianne, and then her mother, Alexandra . . . I used to fancy her. She was a very fine lady . . . Now, so they tell me, he is about to thin out his sons . . . But he pays your salt-money, boy. Until you stop taking it, you are his man. Remember that."

"Yes, Sarge. Thank you."

The outrider reported back. "Three riders ahead, Sergeant. Not horses, camels. They wear strange clothes. Not like our people at all. I didn't get too close. Thought you wouldn't want them to know about us."

The sergeant was jubilant. "Boyo, you've done well. Would they, do you think, be those black-hearted fancy men that came from the East to Jerusalem and set this whole thing going?"

"Can't swear to it, Sergeant." The man grinned in the moonlight. "But I'm betting on it."

"If you're right, you'll be drinking at my expense when we get back to Jerusalem." The sergeant held out his hand. The other riders came close. "Any of you men enjoyed chopping the babies back there?"

No one answered. They, too, were loaded with memories they didn't want.

"That's what I thought. Maybe some of you had fun with the women. I don't know, and don't tell me. Women are one thing, kids are another . . . Anyway, there are three riders on camels some way ahead. Something tells me they could be the funny men who triggered the big party. Personally, I didn't much care for the party. So I say there is a score to be settled. Any objections?"

One man said nervously: "Aren't they under the king's protection?"

"Soldier, you don't keep up with the news. They were supposed to take the brat they were looking for back to Herod. Herod is a great joker. Said he wanted to worship this new king of the Jews. Most likely, the old boy would have done his worshipping with cold steel. Anyway, these wise guys caught on and didn't take the kid back. So Herod blows his mind, and we have to drop all the kids in the area. Joke one, we didn't get the one that mattered. Joke two, the wise guys double-crossed Herod, which he doesn't like too much. So we do Herod a big favour if we take these guys out. It won't take long. After that, we press on with the mission. O.K.?"

The man scratched his head. "If you say so, Sergeant. Will this thing go in your report?"

"Depends," said the sergeant. "Depends on whether we fulfil the mission or not. Herod can be a very funny person. Any questions?"

There were no questions.

"Let's ride, then. Don't do anything until I signal. But when I do signal, make it clean and quick."

They caught up with the Magi sooner than the sergeant had expected. He thought the wise guys might have spotted his troop and made a run for it. But they didn't. They didn't even look back until they heard the sound of hoof-beats on the hard ground. Then they reined in their camels and waited patiently.

"Good evening, sirs," said the sergeant courteously. "You are the very gentlemen who brought news of great importance to King Herod, are you not?"

"We are," said one tranquilly. "Do you have any message for us? We have a long journey to make."

"Sir," said the sergeant, "we are seeking the child you sought. Can you help us?"

In the moonlight, the Persian smiled a silver smile. "I am afraid not. Our mission was a failure. It is sad. We are returning home."

The sergeant also smiled. "Sir, someone must have misled you. You are travelling south. This is the road to Egypt. The road to Persia lies to the north."

"We thank you for this information. Perhaps you would be kind enough to escort us until we reach the correct route."

The sergeant grinned. "Marks for effort, but not on, friend. You are the rearguard. They are taking the kid to Egypt."

The Magi glanced at each other. One of them was reaching for a short curved sword — surreptitiously, he hoped. Another was casually slipping his hand inside his robe. The sergeant noted these movements with some satisfaction.

The one who had already spoken still tried to keep it cool. "Sir, you speak of matters we do not understand. Though I am sure it is not necessary, I beg to remind you that King Herod himself has approved of our journey. He would have given us the protection of his soldiers had we wished it. Now let us go in peace."

The sergeant savoured this moment. "Not on, friend. We found some shepherds. After a bit of encouragement, they talked. We know about you, about the kid you found. About this guy Joseph bar-David and his woman . . . No Herod doesn't like to be crossed. I'm Herod's man, and I can tell you."

The talkative one tried a last throw. "Then may I suggest,

sir, that you escort us to the king? We shall be pleased to explain to him what has happened."

"No, you may not, wise guy. While you make with the funnies, the kid gets to Egypt — and Herod isn't going to laugh too much about that. Also, I got some bad news. You're not going back to Persia, or wherever you came from. You're not going anywhere."

The Magi drew their weapons. Three curved swords — useful for carving, but not for much else — and toy daggers. The sergeant was pleased to see that none of his men had moved. Why the hell should they? They were trained soldiers, all except the boy.

"We are three against five. You may kill us, but some of you will not pass over us. There is still hope for the child of the star."

The sergeant ignored him. "You have a right to know why you are going to die. So I'll tell you and I'll make it fast. If you stupid bastards had kept your mouths shut we wouldn't have had to slaughter a townful of brats, you wouldn't be dying now, and we wouldn't have to chase the one that got away." He spat on the ground in disgust. "Why the hell did you have to tell Herod?"

"We thought he would be pleased to learn of the birth of a great King of the Jews."

The sergeant roared with laughter. "Don't you know that kings — even if they are sane — don't want to know about other kings?" He turned to his troop. "These people want to play with their little swords. I wouldn't give 'em the satisfaction."

"Arrows?" enquired a soldier.

"Arrows," said the sergeant, "and fast."

The Magi tried to manoeuvre their camels, but the clumsy beasts lacked the fast reactions of horses. The sergeant shrugged and motioned to his men. Briskly they took their horses well clear of the camels; and then they reached for their bows.

One of the Magi had begun to charge, but two arrows stopped him, one in the face, one in the chest. He screamed and fell. Before he had stopped threshing about, the other two had joined him on the frosty ground, each transfixed. They rolled about and made horrible noises. The sergeant's professional eye told him that the wounds were mortal.

"Sarge, shall we finish them off?" asked the bumpkin anxiously. He didn't like the noise.

"Why waste arrows? You heard worse than that in Bethlehem. Now we ride south and finish the job."

"Sarge, none of us liked killing the babies back there. Why do we have to go after this one? If you say we chopped it, we'll all back you up. It can't do Herod any harm now."

"Boy," said the sergeant, "there is a nasty logic in human affairs." He gestured towards the dying Magi. "This trash isn't going to stir up more trouble. But what about those shepherds? You want us to go back and take them out? Maybe they already talked to somebody else. Maybe if we let the kid get to Egypt, somebody won't be able to resist telling Herod he wasn't so smart after all . . . No, boy, we ride south and finish the job. We earn our salt-money, and maybe a little extra. I don't like it, but that is the way it is . . . O.K., you soldiers, move!"

One of the Magi was already dead, but the other two were still making sad noises and moving feebly. Steam rose in the cold night air from their death throes. The sergeant didn't look back.

They caught up with the man and the woman and her brat just about dawn. It seemed, somehow, significant.

The sergeant was red-eyed, saddle-sore, dead tired. So were his men. It was a pitiable sight, but the soldiers were too tired for pity.

The woman was riding a clapped-out donkey and trying to breast-feed at the same time. Judging by the squalling, that wasn't working too well. The man was leading the donkey.

He didn't try any rough stuff. How the hell could he? He wasn't armed, his hair was grey, and all he'd got was blisters on his feet.

He just looked at the woman, let out a great sigh and said, "I'm sorry." Maybe there was nothing else to say.

The sergeant said, "You know why we've come."

The man suddenly looked very old. "Yes, we know. . . I have a little money. Perhaps — "

"I'm sorry, friend." The sergeant's voice was gentle. The soldiers hadn't heard him speak gently before. They were surprised. "It has to be done. That mad old king is a mean bastard and he has a good intelligence network. Likely somebody is already following us by now to see that we do the job. So let's get it over with. Herod didn't say anything about killing people — only babies." He turned to the woman on the donkey: "Ma'am, if you give me that child and ride on, I swear to you it will be quick. No pain. I swear it. Then you and your good man can make your way to Egypt and start a new life. You're young. There will be — "

"Monster!" she flared. "Pervert! Murderer! You will kill my child only when I am dead." She clutched it tighter to her bare bosom, and the squalling got louder.

The sergeant didn't seem to know what to do. His men gazed at him expectantly. He was aware of their looks. They were all dead tired and they wanted him to make an end of it.

He turned to the grey-looking man with the blisters, Joseph bar-David. "Look, friend, we are going to pull back a little. Don't think you can make a run for it. But please try to persuade the lady. Make her face reality."

The man looked up at the sergeant. "Is death, then, the only reality?"

"Dammit to hell," exploded the sergeant. "She's your woman! Do the best you can for her. But make her leave the baby, then take her away quickly. We'll wait until you have gone. No pain. I promise."

"What value would *you* place on the promise of a hired killer?"

The man had guts. The sergeant looked at him with respect and, somehow, managed to control himself. "I want no quarrel with you, friend. Just make your good lady see sense, that's all." He turned his horse and motioned to his men. They rode back a little and dismounted.

The bumpkin fingered his bow nervously. "Sarge, why did you let that character give you some lip?"

The sergeant glanced back at Joseph bar-David. He seemed to be pleading with the woman, or reasoning with her. Doing something constructive, anyway.

"Boy, that man is a man. Which is to say that he has courage. He's on a no-win basis. Let him try to sort it out."

"Sergeant," said one of the others, "the woman is taking off. The man is coming at us."

The sergeant sighed. "O.K. They have decided to do it the hard way. Let's get the kid. Mount up."

He hadn't intended to kill the man or the woman, only the baby. But somehow, they all three got killed. And the bumpkin. It happened very quickly.

The bumpkin, being eager, was first in the saddle, first off. The man, Joseph, leaped at him. It was a good leap. It was a great leap. Not what you'd expect from an unarmed man, an old man with grey hair. The bumpkin, taken by surprise, was knocked off his horse and fell badly. The man, Joseph, picked himself up. The bumpkin lay still.

That goddam peasant, thought the sergeant dully. He should have stayed with his sheep. He glanced at the remaining members of his troop and saw that they were overtaking the woman on the donkey fast. He rode at Joseph bar-David.

Again that impossible leap. The sergeant was ready for it, his sword drawn. The horse wasn't. It reared. The sergeant came down on top of the man, Joseph. The sword passed clean through his body and deep into the sand. The sergeant got up groggily. His sword arm hurt. Maybe it was broken. When he could focus he looked down at the dead man. "You poor bastard," he said. "Your goddam luck ran out."

He pulled himself together in time to witness the last act of the tragedy. Some bloody horse soldier — he couldn't see which it was — loosed an arrow at the fleeing woman. She fell from the donkey like a rag doll. The soldier got two for the price of one. The baby was transfixed also.

A little later, there was the reckoning. The bumpkin's neck was broken and so was the sergeant's arm. And there was much blood on the sand where the man had died and where the woman and her baby had died. In death, they all looked very peaceful.

"Who hit the woman?" demanded the sergeant wearily, as someone bound arrows to his arm to stop it flapping about. "No, don't tell me. I don't want to know. It's a bad day. That's all there is to it."

"What about the bodies, Sergeant? Do you want to take that kid back as proof that we — "

"Bury them!" snapped the sergeant. "All together. The bumpkin too. . . Those wise guys — they really started something."

"Well, it's over now."

"Want to bet?" said the sergeant. "Help me get on my horse. It's going to be one hell of a ride back to Jerusalem."

Victoria Regina was riding in the state chariot to her coronation in the temple of Jupiter Capitolinus, still, after all those centuries, the richest, most impressive building in all Londinium. The enduring symbol of the Pax Romana.

It was a fine morning. Many people lined the coronation route. They were cheering well enough. But Victoria knew they were not cheering her. They were cheering the man who rode ahead of her in the gold chariot. The man wearing the imperial purple. Gaius Julius Augustus Germanicus Caesar,

Emperor of Western Europe. The voices in the crowd had been bought by Roman gold — or by British gold that had found its way inevitably by tax and trade to the coffers of Rome.

The Romans had a simple system that worked very well. They did not enslave the people of the lands they had conquered. They gave them 'independence' and protected them — from each other, as the Romans had smilingly explained for centuries. Look, they would say, what Europe was like before the Pax Romana. As if what happened in Europe 1,500 years ago had any relevance to the situation today!

But the Romans — and any jumped-up Italian automatically qualified for Roman citizenship — had it all sewn up. They took their protection money, one-fiftieth of a country's gross national product, and they controlled trade with their subtle tariff barriers. Also they had the big battalions.

Gaius Julius Augustus Germanicus Caesar turned and blew Victoria a kiss. The crowd roared.

Roman gold!

Victoria returned the blown kiss, as she knew she must. She wanted to cry. But the queen of Britannia was not authorised to cry on her way to her coronation. She knew her duty and she could speak fluent Latin. That was all that was required by her master.

Soon he would marry her off to some dreadful German princeling. That much her spies knew of Roman policy.

If only Britannia could be free! Victoria was ambitious for her country. She felt she could make something of it, give it greatness perhaps, if only she had the chance. Why should it remain a poverty-stricken off-shore island whose only destiny was to maintain Roman prosperity? The seamen of this island were the best in the world — even the Romans acknowledged that much. They recruited as many Britannic sailors as possible for their own navy. Given a chance, even half a chance, this off-shore island could become a great sea-power, developing in time its own empire. Perhaps, she thought wildly, it might still be possible to make some kind of alliance with the people of North America, the European refugees from the Pax Romana who were busy forging themselves into a new nation.

Dreams, idle dreams. . . At breakfast, the emperor had hinted that in the not too distant future Rome might mount an expedition to North America before its people became too strong. And before its liberal ideas became too strong.

When Victoria remarked that even the Roman Empire could not hope to last for ever, Caesar gazed at her with tolerant amusement.

"We Romans have an invisible ally, Victoria. So long as he endures, our strength will endure also."

"Who is this powerful ally, Caesar?"

"Jupiter — who else? You know and I know that gods are only ideas and ideals, inventions of the minds of men. But ideas and ideals are powerful weapons. They motivate people, drive them. When we came into Europe, you, all of you, had only weak, tribal gods. Creatures of hate and fear and darkness. The Roman pantheon brought order and light. The tribal gods were defeated by determination and discipline, the ideals given to us by Jupiter. If you could have opposed us with a civilised god or gods instead of the crude imaginings of savage minds, history might have been different. Men will die for a symbol they believe is worth dying for. Our symbol was stronger than any of yours. Jupiter still laughs."

Recalling the conversation as she rode to the empty ceremony in the temple of Jupiter Capitolinus, Victoria realised the truth of what the emperor had said. Gods were symbols, and men craved for symbols. The gods of Europe had not been strong enough for the gods of Rome.

Jupiter still laughed.

And Victoria, shaming herself before her people, wept.

Falcon Chase

NINE DAYS AFTERWARDS, when the machine and the bodies had long ago been claimed by the scientists; when the official reports had been typed out, dispatched and pigeonholed; when the last journalist had drifted away, dully resentful at having got only the *beginning* of the scoop of the century; nine days afterwards, when the incident was already a legend, the three men met to discuss it, each wishing to be convinced by the others that the whole thing was real.

Their cars stood outside The Green Man, a quiet inn six miles out of town on the Falconford road. Nine days ago The Green Man had developed the tense atmosphere of a battle headquarters. But now the excitement was dying — even the landlord was voicing opinions less frequently — and the three men were able, for the first time, to think about it leisurely and in peace.

Sir Alan Leclerc, the chief constable, listened to Inspector Manning as to an equal; while Major Nore sipped his whisky and tried to picture the kind of warfare which once belonged to the more sensational children's comics.

The September twilight deepened. Presently they lost their embarrassment in the intimate glow of a single oil lamp which softened the best room of The Green Man into a lazy ring of shadows. Presently, the men who had dealt solely with facts began to enter the realm of conjecture.

Towards midnight on September 9th a brilliant green shooting star made its appearance remote in the North African sky. It was first seen at Ain Sefra. Later, during the early hours of the morning, it was observed over the Algerian coast, and then the Mediterranean. But unlike most shooting stars, this one did not disappear after a moment or two. Instead, it moved at a high speed in wide circles, yet all the time progressing slowly north. As dawn came nearer, the shooting star was seen above Valencia, Bordeaux, Le Havre and, finally, London.

Then daybreak came, a grey reluctant ghost.

Meanwhile, the alarm bell had sounded at Redmoor Hall Settlement, a large country house which recently had been converted for the accommodation and treatment of criminal lunatics. It was the first time a patient had escaped.

Two hours later, those inhabitants of East Anglia who had switched on their radios heard the eight o'clock news bulletin rapidly become swamped by a sound something like a fast approaching motorboat.

Later reports showed that the interference had been noticed as far north as Dundee.

At ten minutes past eight, the 'motorboating' ceased to interfere with radio reception. At the same time, the people of Cambridge were aware of a brief penetrating hiss, as an indistinguishable but blinding streak of light swept over the city. It was followed by a faintly acrid scent and, a minute or so later, by a miniature whirlwind.

In peaceful fields along the Norfolk border, forty head of placid cattle stampeded. They flattened the hedges and charged along the lanes, to finish up entirely exhausted; some with broken legs and ripped udders.

At quarter past eight, the county police, under the able direction of Inspector Manning, had thrown a patrolling cordon round the four square miles of forest that was Falcon Chase. The inspector, a seasoned hunter of men, hoped to recapture the maniac before midday. He was in a hurry to return to his Norwich burglary; and he was also annoyed that the army, which was using the Chase for an exercise, should have offered to help in the search.

Major Nore was enthusiastic. He gleefully informed the four platoons detailed for the operation that George William Grandiman, besides being a specialist in the destruction of children, was equally expert in the murder of adults. Major Nore also indicated that it was up to the army to recapture Grandiman before the police did. Major Nore also added that he wished the prisoner to be taken alive and uninjured.

The police and the soldiers had begun to close in, truncheons drawn, rifles at the ready but unloaded. The walkie-talkies kept up their monotonous, parrot-wise signals of progress. All this was ordinary procedure for this out-of-the-ordinary job.

But then extraordinary things began to happen.

Major Nore and Inspector Manning, who were busy being consciously polite to each other, were taken unawares by the same blinding flash of light and the loud hiss that had been noticed over Cambridge. The light was lower and brighter, the hiss louder. The consequent whirlwind was more powerful.

A radio operator, standing six or seven yards away from Inspector Manning, seemed to make, without any effort, the jump of a lifetime. He rose forty feet in the air and sailed majestically into the branches of a great oak. He stayed there, hanging in the fork of a thick branch, quite unconscious.

Inspector Manning's respectable black police car was lifted by invisible fingers, turned neatly over and deposited in the middle of the by-road with a depressing crunch. Major Nore's heavy olive-coloured sedan, in spite of its handbrake, was backed into a four foot ditch.

An army dispatch rider, travelling at fifty miles an hour

along the Falconford road, had the frightening experience of being stopped suddenly by an unseen force. He was later found, unable to speak.

The inspector and the major were fortunate enough merely to suffer the indignity of being flattened. When the whirlwind had passed them they lifted their heads and gazed around at the hundreds of trees almost completely stripped of their leaves. At that moment there was a far sound of shattering timbers, and a great wall of flame seemed to hover for a moment, a quarter of a mile away, above the treetops of Falcon Chase.

The inspector and the major looked at each other. This was no time for theories. Major Nore ran to his car, wrenched open the door and hauled out a spare walkie-talkie.

In less than a minute, two platoons of men were moving at the double towards the part of the forest where the flames had been seen.

Thoughts of George William Grandiman and his imminent recapture were eclipsed in Inspector Manning's mind as he raced after the major. With a twinge of self-contempt, he realised that the automatic pistol in his hand was a definite comfort. "What the devil is it?" he panted.

Major Nore stopped for a moment and tried to control his own heavy breathing: "R.A.F. up to some damn thing, I expect. Not surprised at anything nowadays, with all this jet stuff. Better push on, and see if there are any survivors!"

"Did you see anything like a plane?" asked the inspector.

"No," snorted the major, "but I damn well felt it! Same noise, same smell — recognise it anywhere!"

"It made a mess of my car."

"It made a mess of my signaller," said the major drily. "Come on! It's not far now."

They sprinted along between the trees and arrived at the scene a few minutes before the two platoons that had been diverted by Major Nore.

Luckily the forest was very damp after a period of heavy rainfall, and the sudden wall of flame that had been seen by the two men had now died down. It had obviously not started among the closely growing trees, for the boles of those that were still standing were damp and unscarred, while their branches and foliage were black and shrivelled.

An astounding sight met their eyes.

An avenue about two hundred yards long and twenty yards wide had been carved out of the living forest. Dozens of trees had been flattened or bent forward, their roots torn from the earth, as if they were so many matchsticks. At the end of this avenue, its nose buried in earth and broken branches, lay what at first appeared to be a huge silver bullet. It was about ninety feet long and twenty feet in diameter.

Standing in silent amazement behind this extraordinary object, Inspector Manning and Major Nore saw that its rear was a mass of twisted and dully glowing metal tubes. A slight breeze caused something at the side of the machine to move. It appeared to be some kind of door.

"Come on," said the inspector grimly. "Your guess is as good as mine. I think I've seen too many strip cartoons lately!" He walked slowly and purposefully towards the open door, gripping his automatic tightly.

Major Nore followed without comment, his hand firmly holding the butt of his service pistol. At the door they paused.

"This is giving me the creeps. I wonder if there's — anyone at home?" Major Nore was surprised to hear that his own voice had dropped to a whisper.

"Even if there is I shouldn't think they'll be full of joy after a bump like this," replied the inspector quietly. "What do you say — shall we go in, or sing out to them first?"

"Wish my men would hurry up," said the major anxiously. Then, with characteristic decision, he moved ahead of the inspector and scrambled up through the doorway.

The interior was not unlike that of a super trailer, what the salesmen would call 'a functional-living van', except that the materials were strange, the design better, and everything was much smaller.

There were four bunks, each not more than four feet long, which were independently slung from a kind of delicate spider's web of metal. But the metal felt and responded like tough elastic. By the side of each bunk was a panel of switches and instruments, and on the bunk itself a number of thin silver straps. Altogether, the arrangement was a masterly example of shock absorption. Major Nore felt that travelling in them would be rather like lying on three spring mattresses aboard a stratocruiser.

It was only when he had spent thirty or forty seconds gazing about him that he realised there was no source of light. But everything glowed faintly — while contriving not to be luminous. It was as if the quality of light itself had been trapped in the materials of the bunks, the tiny fixed tables and chairs, and all the strange gadgets in the rear compartment. The effect was startling, but pleasant. It was as if the whole cabin were illuminated by some highly developed form of indirect lighting.

The major heard Inspector Manning's voice from outside: "You all right, Major? Anyone on board?"

"Come and have a look," called the major.

Cautiously, Inspector Manning clambered through the doorway.

"Now we've found something for the clever boys to think about!" remarked the major lightly. As he spoke his gaze travelled past the astonished inspector to the nose of the compartment. It was cut off from the rest of the machine by a partition of what looked to be glass. With a stifled exclamation he gripped the inspector's arm and pointed.

The nose compartment was obviously the control room. There were instruments everywhere: large clocks (bearing no terrestrial figures); things like thermometers; a battery of differently coloured switches and buttons; and three large vision screens. In front of the central control panel was an adjustable couch. Across it was sprawled the body of what seemed to be a fair-haired human child.

The two men tried to enter the nose compartment, but the transparent sliding door was jammed. They could only gaze and conjecture. The 'child' was dressed in a flimsy kind of knee-length tunic. It reminded Inspector Manning of the illustrations that are sometimes found in Latin schoolbooks.

"It looks as if his neck's broken." The inspector felt the need to break an uneasy silence.

Major Nore tried desperately to regain a sense of proportion—earthly proportion: "I'll bet the Wright brothers didn't count on anything like this!" He gave a brief, rather forced laugh. He caught the inspector's expression and suddenly became serious. "This is certainly going to be one big headache for the government . . . I wonder where it came from?"

"Well, he can't tell us now." The inspector jerked his head towards the still figure. "We'll have to try and get hold of his companions. They seem to have been in quite a hurry to explore. How long did it take us to get here?"

"Ten minutes," said the major. "Probably less. You don't think there are more of them wandering about the Chase?"

The inspector nodded. "Unless they're hiding in cupboards," he said without humour. "Somehow, I don't think this one would have fancied the trip by himself. And there are the bunks . . . "

Major Nore was completely at a loss. "It's made a mess of your manhunt," was all he could find to say.

"From singular to plural," said the inspector briefly.

The major thought about that. Then he said: "I say, Manning. It's sort of comforting to know they — they're human."

"And little humans, at that," added the inspector with a thin smile.

There were sounds outside. One of the major's platoons had arrived. He immediately got out of the machine and became very military.

"What is it, Major?" The voice of the young 'sub' in charge of the men was filled with excitement and wonder.

"Later!" snapped the major. "Look here, Carslake, I want your men to throw a cordon round this — contrivance. Nobody enters — understand!"

"Yes, sir." Carslake was crestfallen.

"Inspector Manning and I are going to take a look around. Keep position till we come back. Oh, and when Willow's platoon arrives, tell them to begin searching from here, in concentric circles. Tell him — tell him to look for a couple of children, Roman children, as well as Grandiman!"

A constable came running breathlessly between the trees. He stopped still for a moment, his mouth dropping open. Then duty asserted itself, and he made for the inspector.

"The army reports contacting Grandiman, sir. But he bashed one of the soldiers and ran for it."

"Where's this?" asked the inspector sharply.

"South side, sir — two miles away."

"Look here, get to the nearest phone and get hold of the chief constable. Ask him to come here as soon as he can. It's urgent."

"Yes, sir." The constable moved away at a tired jog-trot.

Inspector Manning turned to the major. "We'd better get moving." He gazed speculatively at the great machine behind them. "I rather think I'd like to be in at the first meeting between us and *them*."

Major Nore tried to take the whole thing in his stride. "A good idea," he grunted breezily. "Be something to tell our grandchildren, eh, Manning?"

"If we have any," was the laconic reply.

But it was a man from Willow's platoon who discovered

them first. Major Nore and the inspector, picking their way gingerly among the bracken, heard a great shout of surprise. Then a private came running towards them down a narrow avenue between pine trees.

"Found 'em, sir," he yelled to Major Nore. "Come and have a look!"

The major, who was equally excited, did not stop to discuss the finer points of discipline. It wouldn't have been much use, anyway, for the private, a raw lad, had already turned around and was charging back to a small clearing. Major Nore cast his official dignity to the winds, and took off in pursuit. But the inspector stood there for a few moments, considering the happenings of the past twenty minutes, before he followed.

Major Nore and the private had already disturbed the bodies.

The inspector stood at the edge of the clearing, taking in the whole scene. It reminded him vaguely of the *Wicked Uncles* and the *Babes in the Wood.*

The private looked up: "Their heads have been bashed in, sir. Looks as if Grandiman got here first."

The major stood up a little sheepishly. "Wanted to see what they were really like," he explained, as if in self-defence.

"You shouldn't have disturbed them," said Manning severely, all his professional instincts coming to the fore.

"No need to look for clues, Manning. It's pretty obvious. They've only been gone a few minutes, I should say. Grandiman must have heard us coming, and sheered off."

"My men are working in, and yours are working out," the inspector said almost as if to himself. "So he should get caught between both parties, if it was only a few minutes ago."

He gazed pensively at the two fragile bodies. Inspector Manning did not regard himself as a highly imaginative man: he preferred to leave *that* kind of imagination to the intellectuals of the force. But as he stood there, a grim and vivid picture floated through his mind. He saw these two Romanesque, almost doll-like urchins wandering through this strange terrestrial forest. He saw the look of surprise on their faces when confronted with their first — and last — earthling; a look that must have changed to horror a moment later; a look that was now indelibly set upon their young, curiously innocent faces. He thought of their journey, of the silver machine coursing its silent, unknown miles through the hard and starry darkness to keep a fatal rendezvous.

The inspector stared down at the tiny twisted bodies, the fragile bodies of delicate children. And how the devil did people like this make and use a machine like that? he asked himself. But now he would never know, not till the next time.

A gust of wind brought a few remaining leaves down from the surrounding trees. Some of them fell, a symbolic terrestrial benediction, on the two inert forms. But these two childlike beings from another world were entirely oblivious of the colour, the restless scent, the peculiar beauty of an English autumn.

The chill wind recalled Inspector Manning to his duties. "Let's go and get Grandiman before he gets up to any more tricks," he said tartly. "The blasted maniac has done enough damage for one morning. I bet they stick him back in the mental home and go all psychological on him!" he added bitterly.

"Won't there be a trial for murder?" asked the major.

The inspector glanced at the bodies again. *That* was a nice little problem!

His meditations were suddenly interrupted by a coarse, almost animal cry about a hundred yards away. Then there were sounds of many feet crashing through the forest. Then there was silence.

The major and the inspector gazed at the blank barrier of trees around them.

"Martin, stay here and look after these two until we come back," said the major.

"Yes, sir." The soldier's face was expressionless, but he was not amused. He noticed that the arm of one of the 'children' seemed to be glowing slightly where it lay in the shadow.

"And if Grandiman turns up again," added the inspector, "you needn't be gentle. Make sure you 'bash' first, but not too hard."

"Yes, sir!" The soldier put some enthusiasm into his reply.

As they went vaguely in the direction of the noise, they heard footsteps coming their way. Inspector Manning put a finger over his lips, and stood still. The major did likewise. The other footsteps stopped. The major released the safety catch of his pistol, just in case.

Suddenly there were sounds of running feet, and Lieutenant Willow appeared. He had been tying his shoelace.

"Damn near got a bullet, Willow," said the major angrily, his hopes of a singlehanded, almost singlehanded, capture dashed to the ground.

"Sorry, sir," said Lieutenant Willow.

"You would have been," muttered the major darkly.

"Made any contact with Grandiman?" asked the inspector.

"Oh, him! Yes, we've collared him, sir. I was coming to tell you. He showed fight; I'm afraid he's a little damaged."

"Who got him?" asked Major Nore. "And who damaged him?"

"Sergeant West, sir, performed both operations."

"Good man!"

"I'll have to take charge of him," said the inspector formally.

Grandiman was taken back to the police van on the Falconford road. His face was badly bruised and his forehead was cut but he sat there quietly enough, though every now and then there was a loud crack as he dealt with the hazel nuts he had managed to pick up in Falcon Chase. Already the events of the morning were growing dim in his mind.

It was then that Sir Alan Leclerc, the chief constable, arrived. He gazed at the overturned police car and raised an eyebrow; he gazed at the unconscious signaller who had been removed from the oak; he gazed at the denuded trees, and at the strained faces of Inspector Manning and his companions.

Then Sir Alan said: "You'd better tell me the worst, Manning. I've heard rumours of secret weapons and heaven knows what!"

"The worst is, sir," said Inspector Manning drily, "that we appear to have received a — a spaceship."

"One of ours, I trust," said Sir Alan, with a comfortable after-breakfast laugh.

But the inspector explained briefly, and then took him to see the remains. And after that Sir Alan Leclerc had neither the energy nor the inclination to laugh for many days.

The Prime Minister was informed before ten o'clock. He and the Home Secretary were on the spot before midday. By which time the story had leaked out and, as far as the county police were concerned, hell was let loose.

The newspapers had their fling; and it took a number of very soothing radio talks by a number of eminent men, including the P.M., to persuade the world in general, and Britain in particular, that they were not yet in danger of planetary invasion. Nobody was really convinced, least of all the Prime Minister.

But, unbelievably, after the first hectic excitement it all began to drift into dream dimensions. Presently the headlines grew smaller; the doom prophets simmered down; conversation in the morning trains imperceptibly returned to normal; and the earth continued to revolve placidly along in orbit around the sun.

Because nothing else happened. And finally there grew the comfortable feeling that nothing else would happen . . . until the next time.

The single oil lamp in the best room of The Green Man appeared to Sir Alan Leclerc, after three large brandies, to be a kind of symbol: sanity in a world of drifting shadows.

"It *wasn't* a dream, damn it!" he said indignantly.

"It was not," agreed Inspector Manning, gazing at the dark liquid in his tankard. "I'll tell you what, sir. It seemed as if we were all a lot of characters that had walked into the first act of a play we didn't know."

Inspector Manning, the man who prided himself upon his lack of imagination, had hit the nail on the head. He had expressed not only the feelings of those who had taken part in the brief drama of Falcon Chase, but also the mood of alert bewilderment that had briefly gripped a waiting world.

Major Nore broke the brief silence that followed the inspector's odd remark. "I wonder what the next act will be, and when it will happen?"

Sir Alan gazed into the fire. "Tomorrow, Major. Or the day after. Or the next century, or the century after that. After all, what do we know of *their* time!"

The inspector looked at the chief constable. "Talking of *them*, sir, what did you make of the bodies?"

Sir Alan said slowly: "Somehow, Manning, when I looked at their childlike faces and those — there's only one word for it — those *innocent* eyes, I was reminded of Genesis."

"Don't see the connection, I'm afraid." The major felt it was all becoming a little metaphysical.

"Work it out, Major." The chief constable turned to the inspector again. "By the way, Manning, I had a little talk with Professor Ryles this afternoon. He's willing to stake his reputation that they were at least four hundred years old!"

The inspector digested this information for a moment or two. Then he recalled a vivid picture of autumn leaves falling upon the Babes in the Wood.

"Yes, sir. But not four hundred of *our* years," said Inspector Manning, displaying a wisdom greater than he would ever realise.

Death Watch

THERE WAS A small circular hole in the desert. It looked like a disused well, but it wasn't. Anyone who happened to be wandering around in that barren, desolate waste could walk up to the hole and look at it, anyone at all. But if he happened to be in a mood to disregard the warnings carved in six languages on the smooth stone slabs surrounding the hole, he stood a reasonable chance of being blasted into eternity. For his approach would have been watched by a hundred mechanical eyes, and his movements would have been covered by a dozen different kinds of hidden armament, from self-sighting machine guns to atomic mortars, and from a nest of gas guns to a battery of flame projectors.

For these and other reasons, very few people ever visited the hole; but those who did — chiefly maintenance men — took the precaution of waiting until a hold-fire code signal had been automatically acknowledged by the defence control centre.

The hole ran vertically into the earth, and metal rungs had been set in its side at regular intervals so that a man could descend. Anyone who went deep enough would eventually come to a circular steel trap-door which was illuminated just enough to display the sign: *Comcon Westcom.* It was impossible to open the trap-door except from the inside, for it was simply an emergency exit for *Computer Control Western Command.*

The vast underground room was air-conditioned. It needed to be since the long rows of linked computers were continuously alive and continuously radiating subtle waves of heat. The air was saturated with energy and vibration, yet permanently stale despite its synthetic freshness.

General Guarnerius sat on God's Footstool and gazed up at the circular steel panel directly above his head. Beyond it was the escape chamber and then the trap-door. And beyond that a tunnel to the sky. At idle moments during the course of his long duty watch he had formed the habit of imagining that he stood at the bottom of the escape shaft, gazing up at stars that could be seen even in the daytime from such a vantage point. But he derived more satisfaction from this imaginative transference when he was on night duty: for then he could pretend that he was inhaling the cool scent of the desert, that he was watching the black clarity of space.

God's Footstool, known officially as the Supreme Command Chair, was possibly the most comfortable chair in the world. It was also, in a different way, the most uncomfortable; for none of the men who sat in it were eager to repeat the experience. Generals Guarnerius and Waterman had shared this ordeal with each other — six hours on and six hours off — for the last twenty-nine days. In about another twenty hours their tour of duty would end, and two more generals would assume both the responsibility and the tension. General Guarnerius sighed and resumed his mental countdown of the remaining hours. He felt it would take him several years to learn the art of sleeping once more.

God's Footstool was on a small dais and was surrounded by a semi-circular row of panels. Together they represented the military nerve centre of the entire Western Defence System, their information lights and action studs being linked to thousands of radar and rocket installations streched out over several million square miles. But the nerve centre of the nerve centre was a narrow panel in the middle of the semicircle. It contained thirty small electric bulbs in three rows of ten. The top row — all green — glowed constantly. But the second and third rows — amber and red — were, thank heaven, still dark. At the bottom of the panel were three studs labelled condition Green, condition Amber, condition Red.

For a moment, General Guarnerius allowed his eyes to stray from the control bank and across the great underground nest of computers where he exercised absolute dominion for six hours out of every twelve. There they squatted, the great machines, the tutelary gods of a technological age. Messengers, technicians and programmers were moving purposefully about like priests attending to the esoteric whims and fancies of their strange but powerful deities.

For a moment, Guarnerius saw the whole underground installations as a kind of temple — a temple dedicated to the pursuit of destruction.

And in that moment the game began.

On the panel in front of the general, one green light winked out and one amber light began to glow. At the same time a messenger brought a narrow strip of paper torn from one of the teleprinters.

U.B.O. approaching. Area 2B. Velocity five point two five. North transpolar trajectory. Probable origin Taymyr Peninsula. Probable destination New York area. Triple verified.

Guarnerius gazed unbelievingly at the piece of paper for a moment. He felt he was either looking at a false alarm or a global death warrant. But the words 'Triple verified' eliminated the possibility of a false alarm. Then clearly that unseen chess player on the other side of the world had moved his first lethal pawn.

Automatically, the general switched on both command

microphones, one of which hung loosely round his neck in case of failure by the one built into the control panel.

"Area 2B, first line neutralise. Second and third lines stand by."

The general dismissed his messenger, glanced once more at the slip of paper and spiked it. There were other things to think about now. The approach even of a single Unidentified Ballistic Object placed squarely upon him the responsibility for retaliation. Should he strike now, or should he wait? And if he did wait might not the delay be a strategic error of the first magnitude?

Without looking round, Guarnerius sensed that the great underground chamber and its occupants, human and non-human, were more alive now than ever they had been during the last twenty-nine days. It was as if the entire complex of men and machines had suddenly become his body so that he could feel what was going on even as he could feel the tension in his fingers and every single muscle in his back.

A glance out of the corner of his eye assured him that General Waterman, still wearing pyjamas and looking as if he could use another three hours' sleep, was sitting at the dual control system behind the command dais. Standing orders laid down that two commanders should be available at the first Condition Amber signal. You never knew, one man might drop dead of a heart attack or be seized by a fit of sneezing that could lose a global war.

Standing orders also laid down that the duty command was personally responsible for all decisions, irrespective of consultation. And much as Guarnerius would have liked to discuss the problem of retaliation with General Waterman, not only was there no time, but it was totally unfair to try to split the moral responsibility.

Another messenger came, and almost simultaneously two more green lights winked out and two amber lights began to glow.

The message read:

Ref. U.B.O. Taymyr origin. Missiles affirmative. Chain zero five affirmative. Destination New York affirmative. Area 2B fully engaged. First line one kill. Second and Third lines now striking.

A chain of five missiles, doubtless with hydrogen warheads, all on the same course for New York! Guarnerius suppressed a shudder. It would be a miracle if the second and third defence lines got them all. God help New York.

The general thought briefly of his wife and child in New York, and suppressed the thought immediately.

He spoke into the microphone, surprised at the calmness in his voice: "Ref. Taymyr missiles. Extreme range stations attack conveniently." Then he spiked the message.

Guarnerius tried to imagine all the hundreds of continental defence units that would saturate the Taymyr–New York trajectory with ground to air missiles. It was beyond imagination. He gave it up. The stratosphere would be a screaming inferno of rocket-trails.

Retaliation?

Now, thought the general grimly, when the attack was revealed as an attack without any possibility of error, now was the time to exchange pawns.

He issued the orders: "I.C.B.M. units programmed Leningrad. Shoot five, hydrogen armed. Repeat. Shoot five, hydrogen armed."

And so . . . God help Leningrad.

Two more messengers arrived. Guarnerius glanced at his row of green lights. Only four remained alive. But on the second row six amber bulbs were glowing.

As he took the message slips he spoke once more. "To all united Western Command. Condition Amber. Repeat. Condition Amber."

Then he read the messages.

The first was brief:
U.B.O. approaching. Area 2A. Velocity six point zero. Unverified.

The second was explicit:

Ref. U.B.O. Area 2A. Missiles affirmative. Chain zero five affirmative. Origin Novaya Zemlya affirmative. Destination area Detroit affirmative. Triple verified.

The general's throat was dry, dry and tight. It would be a hell of a joke now if he lost his voice, a hell of a joke.

But he didn't lose his voice: "Ref. Novaya Zemlya missile chain. Area 2A all lines neutralise. Extreme range stations attack conveniently."

Guarnerius thought vaguely of that impossible chess board and of his distant adversary. Queen's pawn to Queen Four. Soon it would be time to deploy the bishops and then the knights. Or perhaps one should strike out with the Queen and try for Fool's Mate . . .

The green lights on the centre panel were all dark now. The missile attack was developing swiftly, with transpolar and transatlantic chains converging on a number of targets. The messengers were arriving, one after another, almost without pause. And the intolerable decisions had to be made, one after another, almost without pause . . .

Attack, check and counter-attack. Swarms of missiles were now hurtling towards New York, Detroit, Chicago, San Francisco, Washington. Ground to air missiles were rising by the hundred in fast, optimistic cones of interception. And more missiles were on their way to Leningrad, Moscow, Kharkov, Odessa and the great cities of the East.

Everywhere Death was in transit at thousands of miles an hour. Everywhere Death rode the stratosphere; and presently the first city would endure a bright arrow of darkness from the air.

For General Guarnerius, God's Footstool had become a throne of fire. He wished — he wished stupidly, impotently that he had never been born.

Another messenger came. One of the amber lights died and a red light began to glow.

Guarnerius read the words, and his heart was ravaged by a bleak and silent cry. New York was dead. The fifth missile in the first chain had delivered its cargo of darkness.

New York, the proud city, a pawn less on the planetary chess board.

The destruction was insane, but the logic of insanity was more durable than the logic of love or fear or forgiveness. The destruction would continue until there was nothing left to destroy, until the will to destroy was itself broken.

One cannot play chess with cities, he thought, for cities are people, good or bad, sublime or ignoble, and people are the sacred temples of life. Then he thought: this is no attitude for a soldier. A soldier is profane.

And suddenly he reached his decision. Let the final profanity do what it could to save something somewhere. Not to win a war, or to lose it. But just to save something. For if the destruction continued on the level of planetry chess nothing could be saved, nothing at all. Therefore the concept of chess would have to be abolished, and the totality of destruction exhausted, or itself destroyed.

General Guarnerius issued his instructions, and noted with clinical detachment that there was not the slightest tremor in his voice: "To all units Western Command: Condition Red. Repeat. Condition Red. To all strike units programmed for Eastern targets. Shoot five, hydrogen armed. Repeat. Shoot five, hydrogen armed."

And, he added silently, may God have mercy on the soul of man.

The messengers had begun to arrive in twos and threes now. New York was now no more than the first name on an expanding casualty list.

Guarnerius felt the futile guilt turn deep inside him like a white-hot knife. For he and his adversary on the other side of the world were, between then, trying to annihilate a million years of evolution; and, between them, were consuming the radiance of man in a fire that because it was not divine could only be the product of minds so intellectually arrogant as to be made of the very stuff of hell.

Suddenly Guarnerius realised that he and his adversary were the loneliest, most despicable human beings on the planet. It was a grim distinction. He knew now that he no longer wanted to live.

At that moment the sound of the Cease Fire Bell seemed to explode in his ears. The bell was linked to a short-wave radio circuit that could only be activated by the President or his deputy. At the same time an ultra-priority message was slipped into his hand.

It read:

President direct to C.C. Western Command. Terminate offensive action. Negotiations pending. Tallboy.

The message had to be authentic, since Tallboy was the codeword known only by the President, Waterman and himself. A different codeword was used for each tour of duty.

And yet sabotage was not impossible . . .

Guarnerius had to make his mind up fast. There was no time to analyse the possible diplomacy of negotiating over two continents that were on the brink of annihilation. There was no time to decide between idiocy and futility. There was no time to think.

"All units Western Command," called Guarnerius evenly into the microphone. "All units Western Command. Condition Green. Repeat. Condition Green. Destroy present attack missiles only. Repeat. Destroy present attack missiles only. Terminate retaliation. Repeat. Terminate retaliation."

And then there was another decision that had to be faced. By this time more than half the missiles of Western Command would be streaking through the blue-black outer sky towards their Eastern targets. His Condition Red directive had seen to that. The problem was, should those still within destruction range, and that would be practically all, be eliminated or allowed to continue? If they were allowed to continue, they would doubtless negate all possibility of an armistice. If they were destroyed, Western firepower would be so weakened that, if an armistice failed, capitulation would probably follow.

It was an intolerable decision. But then life itself was intolerable.

"To all strike units. Cancel Eastern target shoot. Repeat. Cancel Eastern target shoot. Destroy all airborne missiles. Repeat. Destroy all airborne missiles. Resume Condition Green. Repeat. Resume Condition Green."

So that was that!

For a few moments General Guarnerius was aware of absolute silence. The death of death. Then he heard the subdued hum of the machines once more, the excitement and exclamations in a background that was far, far away. He glanced at the circular steel panel above his head, and thought of its tunnel to the sky. But now, he thought, the sky was no longer dark and clean. It was distorted and contaminated by all the red trails of madness that had swept across it.

Glancing at his panel clock, Guarnerius saw that the war had lasted fifty-five minutes. A long, long lifetime. He tried not to think of the millions who had died. Not Western or Eastern citizens, only human beings. He tried not to think of them, but the attempt was useless.

If only this damned racial suicide had started the day after tomorrow. If only he, too, could have been up there on the surface, vaporised with the rest of the anonymous dead.

He realised that a hand was resting on his shoulder. He realised that General Waterman was talking to him.

"Welcome," said Waterman gently. "Welcome to the fraternity of the damned."

"Is it really over?" asked Guarnerius. But he knew that everything was over, only there was nothing else to say.

"It's over. Soon you'll be back in New York, sleeping it off for a year."

Guarnerius thought he was mad. "There is no New York."

"Take it easy. New York is O.K. So is Detroit, Leningrad and Moscow. This is your first tour of duty. Everybody gets Operation Try-out on the first tour." Waterman gave a crooked smile. "I had mine eighteen months ago. I thought I'd go insane. But I didn't."

"Operation Try-out! What the hell do you mean?"

"It's one thing to sit waiting for it on God's Footstool," said Waterman quietly. "And it's another thing to suddenly find that you are the left hand of God. We have to know how everyone who sits in the Supreme Command Chair is going to react. So we switch in a computer-cooked simulated war. Next time your duty comes round, you'll be watching some other poor bastard torturing himself to death . . ."

General Waterman paused. Guarnerius looked as if he wanted to say something. He did, but the shock was still too great, and somehow he couldn't quite fit the words into his voice. His mind had been obsessed with the numberless dead; and so the revelation hit him with the weight of a hundred million reprieves.

"The cloak and dagger boys say the East has pretty much the same system," went on General Waterman. He was talking chiefly for the sake of talking, giving Guarnerius time to readjust.

"It's a good technique, apart from the value of the reaction statistics. Nobody who's been through this kind of hell once is going to be trigger-happy in a real Condition Amber. Not here and not in the East." He chuckled. "In fact, so far as I can see, the end product is going to be a corps of international military pacifists."

But General Guarnerius wasn't listening. He was filled with a great emptiness; and then suddenly — though he was not one who had much patience for religion — he was filled with a sensation deeper, more powerful, even more humble than prayer.

For life was still for the living, and the earth still wholesome, the air still sweet. And somewhere — not in time or space — he heard a small bird singing.

The Life and Death of Plunky Goo

I'LL TELL YOU what it feels like to be hated by millions of children. It feels cold. You can sit in front of a fire, drink half a bottle of whisky or go sunbathing on the Riviera — and it still feels cold. But in time you can get used to practically anything, even that. I know: I did. And now I don't even have nightmares any more. Well, hardly ever . . .

Besides, if I get a little depressed now and then, there's always the one unfailing remedy. I just start walking. I've been doing that for the last five years, and I've covered something like ten thousand miles. It's very soothing, is walking. Better than any kind of psychoanalysis you can buy. I ought to know because I've tried both. But walking does something for you that psychoanalysis can never do: it takes you away.

A man I used to know once said: "You can buy respect with a Bentley, but you can only buy self-respect with a Rolls." At that time I had a Rolls and a Bentley; but I can't remember having any self-respect. Only a five-figure income, a country house, a town flat, two ex-wives and Plunky Goo.

You don't remember Plunky Goo? That makes me very happy indeed. But the children still remember. I know because I keep asking them. My only remaining ambition is to live long enough to find that all the children have completely forgotten.

They will in time. But Plunky Goo is a persistent little chap. He follows me everywhere, trotting along like a tiny toy dog at my heels. I don't suppose you can see him. Nobody else can. But he's there just the same.

And he isn't a toy dog. He's a hand puppet, with a face full of mischief and love, just like an intelligent bush baby. And he has a wonderful little voice, just right for whispering secrets, the kind of secrets that are designed to brainwash millions of trusting children.

It was all right when I was just a small-time ventriloquist with no wider audience than a select children's party or Christmas Eve at the orphanage or the bucket and spade set at the seaside.

Those were halcyon days when Plunky Goo only told them the kind of secrets *they* wanted to hear. I didn't make much money but I was happy.

The trouble was Plunky Goo was good. He was very good. He could make the sick ones smile and the healthy ones sick with laughing. I'd spent years working out the technique so that I'd got to thinking exactly as a child thinks and knowing exactly what a child wants. And Plunky Goo would stare at them with his wide bush baby eyes and tell them the kind of silly things that only children can understand, and presently you couldn't have broken the trance with anything less than a hand-grenade.

Yes, Plunky Goo was good, though I say it myself. He was too good. Looking back, I can see that the television trap was practically unavoidable.

At first it was only a five-minute spot on the 'Tea Time For Tinies' programme. This, I thought, was the opportunity for him to give more happiness to more children in one quick shot than in all his other performances rolled together. I prepared for that programme carefully; and Plunky Goo delivered a concentrated dose of the best techniques I'd ever used. He was more than a success: he was a smash hit, humdinger, whamo and sockeroo. He was the tops. The fan mail began to arrive in sacks.

After that there was a weekly spot: then eventually a daily spot. And the viewing figures leapt clean off the top of the graph like a scalded cat.

At which point, the admen got me. It was a good old-fashioned ambush, the kind that hardly ever fails. There was a party somewhere, and somehow I was at it. Quite by chance I met a man who knew a man who thought that Plunky Goo was the biggest thing since fairies. Presently there were three of us in a quiet room away from the party, and I had a magic whisky glass that never got empty; and the third man was explaining carefully how Plunky Goo could fulfil a vital social function by persuading the dear kiddies and their mums to get the best out of life in a world of clean, easy living. And pretty soon there was a fountain pen and a big contract with small print and a cheque that looked like a fair estimate of the nation's gold reserve.

It was quite a long time before I woke up stone cold sober because I'd discovered that the world seems rather pleasant when you look at it through a rosy financial haze. And by then Plunky Goo time had been properly launched.

The admen were having a Roman carnival, and two or three million infant consumers were steadily blackmailing their mums into buying almost every product that could be endorsed by a hand puppet made out of fur fabric, papier-mâché and two plastic buttons.

Sales figures followed viewing figures and soared right out of the graph. Breakfast cereals, offering one model Plunky Goo for twelve packet tops, were actually sold by the dozen; and retailers and supermarkets were cleaned out on the day of delivery. Plunky Goo toothbrushes spread liberally with pink Plunky Goo toothpaste brushed a hundred million infant teeth twice a day, seven days a week all because of an imitation bush baby face and an insane confidential whisper.

Plunky Goo biscuits, Plunky Goo custard, soap, sandals, vests, tricycles, cots, prams, carpets, wallpapers, jellies and ice-cream blocks were invincible. They knocked the opposition absolutely flat. One manufacturer of Plunky Goo plastic panties actually shot himself because, after half a dozen endorsements, one month's orders exceeded his maximum output for the next two years.

Shares rocketed and shares fell through the floor. Plunky Goo may not have caused an actual panic on the Stock Exchange, but he certainly tripled the sales of aspirin in the City.

And what was I doing while all this was going on? For fifteen minutes every day I was the voice of Plunky Goo. For the rest of the time I was engaged in the difficult task of trying to spend money faster than I made it. The days, weeks, months and years began to pass me by as if I were a perpetual sleepwalker.

I never dreamed it was possible to have it so good until the day I suddenly woke up and realised what Plunky Goo had been doing to the nation's children. I still don't know how it happened. Maybe I'd just got bored with being rich and sleeping with my head stuck in a pile of de luxe sand. Or maybe I'd simply got that morning-after feeling, because it happened to be the morning after my second wife had left me.

But I took a long hard look at Plunky Goo and I didn't like what I saw. No longer was he the little friend whose silly secrets and clumsy humour set children free — if only for a few minutes — from all the tiny tremendous problems of childhood. Plunky Goo had changed. He had become a demanding god who spoke only what the high priests of the admen wanted him to speak. He had become a god who demanded worship and sacrifice. Human sacrifice and the abdication of free will.

The truth hit me like a hammer.

And then the telephone rang. Somebody began to talk about a big new deal. A political deal. It seemed that somebody had decided that if Plunky Goo could control seven per cent of the parents then he could certainly control the coming general election. I put the phone down while somebody was still talking. I just wanted to be sick.

Plunky Goo for Prime Minister! Plunky Goo for Archbishop! God save our gracious Plunky Goo!

In a moment of clarity I saw that Plunky Goo could do almost anything, almost anything the admen wanted. He could even become immortal and sit on the high throne of purchasing power for ever. Unless . . .

That afternoon when I went to the studio I went with murder in my heart and murder already on my conscience. I felt that I was the greatest mass exterminator the world had ever known. The others had only managed to destroy bodies, but I was helping to destroy souls.

Transmission began. And for five minutes Plunky Goo went through his routine while I stared at the teleprompter and whispered loaded bush baby secrets to millions of innocent bush baby minds. Then suddenly I could do it no more.

I snatched the glove puppet off my hand and bellowed: "Look, children, Plunky Goo is nothing but cloth and cardboard!" Then, before the astounded cameramen could cut me out, I tore that insidiously lovable Plunky Goo to pieces with my bare hands. I crushed his head between my fingers, and I cried aloud with joy. "Now he's dead!" I shouted. "He's dead, children. And you'll never see him again!"

Then I walked out of the studio and just kept on walking. And I've been walking ever since.

It was a sensation. The death of Plunky Goo was headline news in all the newspapers and even rated a fourth leader obituary in *The Times*. The admen, in a uselessly vengeful mood, tried to get me declared insane. But, thank heaven, it was still a free country. Plunky Goo in his short but riotous life had not had time to corrupt the blind goddess.

Eventually the panic died down. The Plunky Goo sponsors went into mourning and their rivals into increased production. Plunky Gooism was finished and out of its ashes there rose a new era of private enterprise.

As for me, I was waiting to see the casualty figures, only no one but me would have recognised them as such.

And no one at all would ever be able to estimate the final price of freedom. Not unless they had access to the private records of every child psychiatrist, doctor, school teacher and probation officer.

But, during the next few weeks, there were more small children killed on the roads than at any previous period. There was also an epidemic of mysterious falls from first-, second- and third-storey windows. And the number of misadventure verdicts for children consuming sleeping tablets, pain relievers and pep pills was sufficient for questions to be asked in the House and new legislation to be introduced for the control of dangerous drugs.

These were my casualty lists. These were the children who could not survive the destruction of their godhead—the children who had to die so that other children could be free.

But worse than the reproach of the dead was the hatred of the living. I could feel the hatred of all those children following me wherever I went, whatever I did. And it's something I shall have to bear until there are no more children left who remember.

Because even if I could contact them all I couldn't explain why Plunky Goo had to be destroyed. No one could. How could you possibly convince any normal child that a large number of kind, well-meaning, friendly adults — many of them parents themselves — wanted to wave Plunky Goo like a magic wand and transform children everywhere into miniature automatic buying machines?

Children have too much faith in adults to believe stuff like that. They are clean and honest and trusting. They will only hate an adult if they can't find any possible way of avoiding it.

And that's why I keep on walking. Because, you see, being a tramp is the next best thing to being a ghost.

The Menhir

THE TRIBES CAME from the north and from the west. Every year, at the time of the winter solstice, they made their long and hazardous journeys into the desert. Every year they came to visit the Sightless One. Every year they came to conduct the ancient ceremony of Searching Out.

The desert itself was a curiously dead land. Nothing could live there for very long — not even the most hardy animals — because of desert sickness. So, once the ceremony was over, the tribes packed up their tattered tents and departed hurriedly to live in relative peace of mind for another four seasons. But, even so, the days began to pass and the peace of mind grew less until everyone's thoughts turned hypnotically once more to the next Searching Out, the next count of the Perfect Ones and the dismissal of the Changelings.

As she walked with her tribe, the People of the Spur, on the last day's march towards the rendezvous, Runa felt the weight of the fear inside her far more than the weight of the small child slung over her shoulder. Runa was seventeen years old and her baby son, Thali, a mere three seasons. This was his first Searching Out. It was also likely to be his last.

When Runa was fifteen, her village had been attacked one night by a group of escaped Changelings, the wild, grotesque creatures who lived mainly in the hills and were shunned by all ordinary people. They had killed many of the Spur menfolk and stolen many of the women. Runa was among those taken. Eventually, however, she had managed somehow to break out of the cage in which they kept their prisoners — though not until they had already got her with child — and made her way back to the village.

Being wise for her years, she took the simple precaution of lying immediately with two or three of the Spur men, so that when Thali was born none could claim with certainty that he was a child of the Changelings. Fortunately, apart from a long thin weal across his back, there was nothing wrong with the baby at all; and so he was not dismissed at birth.

Only Runa saw that as the baby grew, so the weal grew into a raised ridge from which sprouted thick red hairs. She took care to keep him well covered, pleading a weakness for chills and fevers. But presently the ridge grew big enough to be felt through the coarse cloth in which he was wrapped. In desperation, Runa took to scraping it with a sharp stone in the still of the night. Pieces of it flaked off, but then new segments grew to take their place. The task was impossible; and besides there was the added difficulty of keeping the child's mouth stuffed with rags to deaden his crying.

It was, of course, a futile gesture; for at the Searching Out, Thali would be presented naked for inspection — like every other man, woman and child of the lawful tribes — at the foot of the Sightless One. Then the priests would discover his imperfection. Then he would be dismissed. And his tiny body would be tossed upon the monstrous cairn that yearly grew into a bleached and terrifying mountain.

Runa was a fatalist, but no simple fatalist. She knew that in the end Thali must die; and knew too that she must do all she could to save him. For that, also, was ordained.

Now, the tribe was less than a day's march from the rendezvous; less than a day's march from death. Tonight, they would make camp with the other tribes in the greenly glowing desert only a few bowshots from the foot of the Sightless One. And tomorrow, before dawn, the priests would lead their people to the Searching Out. And when the Sightless One's shadow touched the hill of bones, the slaughter would begin.

Runa was tired and depressed and almost oblivious of her surroundings. Mechanically, she continued to place one foot before the other, vaguely aware of the background chatter and the whispered anxieties of the other women as they followed the groups of menfolk. Now and again she managed to make some automatic response to the odd remark that was addressed to her; but for the most part she walked in a shroud of loneliness, knowing only that the red sun was bending low towards Thali's last sunset.

Later, when the camp had been set up, when the communal meal had been eaten and the fires had burned to dull embers, she lay with Thali in the lee of a massive boulder and gazed sleeplessly at the clear night sky.

The constellations were pricked out in immobile brilliance. But Runa did not know much about stars. She supposed that they were nothing more than a sprinkling of frozen fire-dust, no doubt as unhealthy to be near as the fire-dust that was carried by the winds of earth. Sometimes it drifted against the walls of huts or tents, until there was a tiny glowing pile that had to be swept away before everyone got dust sickness.

Runa gazed at the stars and then at the sprawling cluster of tribal tents in the immense dead sea of the desert. Suddenly she wanted to run away; though to do so would be to meet death just as surely as Thali would meet the dawn blade at the foot of the Sighless One. For the desert hated life and all that was living; and none could hope to escape its evil alone.

For a moment or two, Runa considered the possibility of asking one of the Spur people to go with her — a boy barely her own age who had lain with her several times. But then she pushed the thought out of her mind; for if he refused, he would doubtless stop her escape also, or else give the alarm when she had gone.

Having made her decision, Runa stood up, holding the now sleeping child tightly to her body. Then she crept quietly and almost without breathing from the camp. Evidently no one had seen her departure; and when she had covered perhaps the distance of a long bow-shot, she came to a halt and let out a long sigh of relief.

Thali was still asleep. Gently she eased his small half-starved body into the shoulder sling that all the women used for carrying their babies. The problem now was where to go. But there was nowhere to go; for the desert was all around her, patchily glowing with the dull green of death.

It might have been possible to retrace the route taken by the tribe. But that was more than three days' march, and she had neither food nor water. So it did not really matter which direction she took.

In the end, noticing a bright yellow star that hung low on the horizon, she decided to follow it. It looked a much warmer and friendlier star than the others. And in any case, it was too far away to be poisonous. Runa hitched Thali into a comfortable position and started to walk.

The desert was a place of ghosts; but the ghosts were older even than the tribes. They were as old, so Runa knew, as creation itself. They were part of creation; and they whispered to each other in words that no one living could understand. As she walked, Runa heard their whisperings and was surprised that she was not more terrified. Perhaps, she told herself bitterly, it was because she had learned that there was more to fear from men than from ghosts.

The desert was also a place of glowing sands, of strangely dancing lights, of clouds of fire-dust, of rocks that were smoother than ice yet harder than iron. There were rivers of stone veined with all the colours of the rainbow and dry pools of powdery blackness that stirred and rippled like restless water. Truly, it was a wilderness indeed.

Runa found it hard to follow the yellow star. She struggled across gullies and hillocks, grazing her feet and legs on sharp unseen stones. After a time she began to regret her folly. Surely it would have been better to let them take Thali from her? But then she knew it would not. The child belonged to her. It was the only living thing that had ever belonged.

Immersed in her thoughts, she saw the narrow black chasm at her feet a moment too late. The despairing cry she gave as she fell was driven from her body by a great hammer blow between the shoulders. She could not breathe, could scarely move. The child was jammed tight against her and the two of them were wedged between the narrowing, dreadfully smooth surfaces of rock.

Thali had not moved or made any sound. Clearly he was dead; for the pressure of his thin little body against hers seemed enough to snap her ribs. As she tried to breathe, Runa could hear the rattling air forced from her baby's mouth by the painful pressure of her own chest.

This was a judgment. She had tried to save Thali from the Searching Out and so she had been condemned to kill him herself.

Fortunately the chasm was not deep. As she writhed in pain and tried desperately to ease the terrible pressure, Runa's toes touched the bottom. Working in agonising haste against the clouds of unconsciousness that threatened to swallow her, she managed at last to ease the child's limp body round to her side. And after a time the pain in her arms and chest subsided.

Runa looked up and saw a mistily dancing pattern of stars framed by the lip of the chasm, no more than an arm's length above her head. Presently the stars became still, and she was able to think clearly once more.

She took the tattered cloth shoulder sling in which she had carried Thali and tore it into strips, knotting them together. One end of the rope she tied tightly round the baby's motionless form and the other she gripped between her teeth. Then she began to climb by the simple process of forcing her back against one side of the fissure and her feet against the other.

Twice she fell; but at the third attempt she succeeded in mustering the tremendous effort needed to haul herself out knowing that she did not have enough strength for another try. As soon as she reached the surface, she pulled the child's body quickly after her, bumping it from side to side, desperate with the need to hold it tenderly in her arms.

She gripped the pitiful bundle to her, smothering it with kisses and meaningless soothing sounds. Then suddenly the stars fell out of the sky, the desert dissolved and she was sucked down into a whirlpool of darkness.

When at last Runa opened her eyes once more, it was in the ghost-grey light of pre-dawn. And there before her loomed the grim stone shape of the Sightless One.

She gave a cry of anguish. Was it for this that she had faced the terrors of the desert? Was it for such awful disobedience, for such blasphemy of thought and deed, that the Sightless One had doomed her to kill her own child?

For the first time in her life, Runa was no longer afraid of the Sightless One. His monstrous, god-like implacability had become too great for fear.

Still holding Thali she leapt to her feet and gazed defiantly at the sand-smoothed stone column. It rose massively, twice a man's height from the desert, as if the still recognisable man-shape stood upon a great finger of rock whose base might rest at the very centre of the earth.

"Take what must be taken, then!" cried Runa. "And take with it the curse of every such woman, of every such child between earth and sky. Kill me if you can, for my heart is sick, and there is nothing now to love, and I wish to die."

Then she flung Thali at the foot of the Sightless One, and flung herself beside him, thankful that this was at least an end.

It was indeed an end. But the end was tricked out as a beginning.

Suddenly, the baby uttered a great sigh. It began to whimper. Before Runa's astounded eyes it tried to sit up.

The rags in which it had been wrapped were almost torn from its back. And across the shoulders and spine there were ugly bruises and some small cuts. Across the spine also there was a weal — of pink new skin, with fragments of horn and hair clinging to it like the remains of a monstrous scab.

Thali's whimpering gathered power until it became a lusty howl. And Runa sobbed with joy. Glancing up at the Sightless One, still impassive and immobile, there rose inside her a song without words or understanding.

Her child was alive and — as she pulled away the last remaining traces of horn and hair with her fingers — demonstrably a Perfect One. The new skin was bleeding a little from the ordeal in the chasm and from her own impatient fingers. But no matter. Thali would pass the Searching Out.

She would think of some excuse for going alone into the desert, and she would tell of the accident; and all would be well. And presently the old men would weave a new legend . . .

Already the tribes were approaching for the ceremony. She could see them winding towards the Sightless One across the desert, ghost-grey columns in a ghost-grey world.

She turned to look once more at the stone monument — impassive and immobile. The timeless god of time, the fearless god of fear, the deathless god of death.

Now, with unformed images of miracles and mercy tumbling through her mind, Runa began to feel that such a godhead could not be completely immune to love. And perhaps, in the end, the message of love would be made communicable. And in the space of generations grow into a new vision that would cast out fear and transcend the need of death.

But the Sightless One knew nothing of the troubles of the living, or of the need for compassion in a world made harsh by men. A world of sickness and hope, of courage and desolation, the legacy of a race that brought about its own destruction on the far side of the centuries.

For the Sightless One was no more than the strangely enduring monument to a man who had once been as other men. One who had sailed seas now shrouded in history. One who in battle had lost an eye and an arm, and finally a life. One who had gained the brief immortality of fame and the more enduring immortality of stone.

Long ago, the Sightless One had stood on a high stone column in the square of a great city, where fountains played and pigeons squabbled and effigies of couchant lions kept their solemn vigil.

But now the lions were buried under the patchily glowing sands of a man-made desert, the fused and blackened remains of the city were entombed for ever in silence. And all that remained on the surface of a world that refused entirely to die was a thinly enduring courage and — sometimes — the tender miracle of love.

The Doomsday Story

It is now August 31st, 1965 and my job is finished. Tomorrow, after the press conference and the farewell dinner and the television appearance and what-have-you, I shall, I hope, be able to retreat into total personal obscurity. A man can only enjoy being headline news for so long; and in my case the time limit is measurable in hours. After that, notoriety becomes nothing more than an endurance test.

Heaven knows how the prima donnas of film and television stand it, or even the teenage wonders who seem to stay in the spotlight only long enough to collect their Jaguars and share certificates. Perhaps they have tougher constitutions, or perhaps I'm just a shade more sensitive. Anyway, five years have been rather more than enough; and I'm glad that it's all over.

Not that — publicity apart — they have been uneventful years. I have survived three assassination plots, two attempted kidnappings and an invitation to 'escape' to the Soviet Union where, it was promised, I would be able to live happily ever after as a proletarian millionaire, providing I did just enough atomic research on the side to make things look decent. And, of course, during the last five years I have received about half a million 'fan' letters, the ratio of utter disgust to complete approval being something like five to one.

But I had better begin at what, though it is certainly not the beginning in any reasonable sense of the word, is the point where I — as it were — stepped upon the stage and pirouetted before the footlights.

In April 1960, after some time at Harwell and a couple of years on a pleasant little island installation which is still mistakenly classified Top Secret, I was regarded as a very promising sub-atomic physicist. Not, perhaps, as good as Wilhoff Rausen or even Jenkins at Cambridge, but still — as the Americans would say — in the big league. Besides, as far as the government was concerned, I was supposed to have qualities which would make me more suitable for the project in hand than any of the people I have mentioned.

I was supposed to be ruthless and ambitious, though how this reputation came to be pinned to me I have no idea. Perhaps it had something to do with the rumour that I had married a niece of the Minister of Science in order to push Blue Strike as a vehicle for a neat little atomic warhead that my team had devised. However, although I must admit that I did actually marry one of the Minister's delightful nieces, Blue Strike had already gone the way of all missiles by that time. So I can only maintain my attitude of injured innocence.

But, whatever the reason, I was picked as the man for the job. Consequently, one delightful spring afternoon in 1960, I had a most fertile tea-time conversation with the Prime Minister, the Minister of Science *and* the Chancellor of the Exchequer.

The atmosphere was friendly, informal. The M. of S. called me Richard and enquired dutifully after my non-existent children (he has so many nieces); the P.M. called me Hamilton and wanted to know if I was interested in shooting; and the Chancellor, without calling me anything at all, tactfully tried to find out how interested I was in money.

But presently, after a few preliminary skirmishes, the Prime Minister came to the point. "We have a new job for you,

Hamilton," he said bluntly, "on what will certainly be the most important and, I may say — " his eyes flickered momentarily into a canine smile — "the most controversial scientific project of our time. Are you interested?"

"More than interested, sir. I am agog."

The smile flickered once again. "If you can pull it off successfully, a knighthood will be the least of your numerous rewards."

Sir Richard Hamilton — possibly O.M. The prospect intrigued me. Not that I'm essentially snobbish, you understand. But for some inexplicable reason I have always seemed to experience difficulty with head waiters. A knighthood was the sort of thing that was likely to improve restaurant facilities considerably.

"You can pick your own team," said the M. of S. encouragingly, "and you will have an A-plus priority on materials and equipment."

I thought for a moment. "What is the classification of work, sir?" I asked. "Secret or open?"

"Both," answered the M. of S. "The project will be declared, but all aspects of the work—research, construction, trials, progress, success or failure — will remain Most Secret."

"There will be watch-dogs?" I enquired.

"Barking in great profusion," confirmed the P.M. soberly.

"You will have unlimited financial resources," went on the Minister of Science.

"Figuratively speaking," put in the Chancellor quickly.

"In fact, all that we ask," concluded the M. of S., "is that you give us some reasonable hope of success."

I gazed at the three of them a little incredulously. Even allowing for the normal subtlety of the political mind and the slight reservations concerning personnel, equipment and finances that would doubtless be revealed at a later stage, I was being offered what amounted to the scientist's vision of paradise. There had to be a flaw, of course; and as I had not yet been told exactly what they wanted me to do, that was obviously the flaw.

"Gentlemen," I said, "before we go any further let me say that I unhesitatingly accept. And I will certainly do my best to assure a reasonable hope of success."

They looked surprised.

"But you don't yet know what is required," said the P.M.

"With the facilities you are offering, sir, it can hardly be anything less than the so-called Doomsday weapon."

The three men sat bolt upright and gazed at me suspiciously. *"How did you know?"*

I didn't know, but it was not the time to admit to inspired guesswork. So I rationalised on the basis of a technique originated by the late Sherlock Holmes.

"It was quite simple, really. I am a reasonably good subatomic physicist; but there are better ones, and therefore you must already know that the better ones would not be interested in this project, probably on moral grounds. Therefore the project must be a weapon. But we already possess atomic weapons of multi-megaton calibre. Little further research is needed on these and also their production costs can be worked out reasonably accurately. However, you are offering me priority research facilities and as much money as I need. So you want something rather more lethal than a dozen or two hundred-megaton bombs. Which brings us to the Doomsday machine, which is as yet no more than an unholy nightmare."

"Is it possible?" asked the P.M.

I shrugged. "Would you have said thermonuclear bombs were possible thirty years ago?"

"The Americans seem to think it's possible," said the Minister of Science despondently. "Therefore the Russians will undoubtedly take it seriously. So we must do something about it, too."

I looked at the Prime Minister. "Will you tell me one thing, sir? What would be the practical value of a machine or weapon that is designed not only to obliterate the enemy but also the rest of the human race?"

The P.M. looked suddenly grey and tired. "Inestimable. Not only would it take the theory of balance of power to its absurd conclusion, it would also stand a good chance of lifting diplomacy out of the depths of blackmail and restoring it once more to the realms of negotiation."

I thought about that for a moment, then I said cheerfully: "I don't really know whether or not it's possible to construct a Doomsday weapon, but I'll do my damndest, sir."

Oddly enough, that didn't seem to make the three of them any happier at all.

Things began to move pretty quickly after that. As I had been given A-plus priority, I made pretty extensive use of it. I am a northerner by birth, and it occurred to me that it would be rather pleasant to work in one of the Derbyshire valleys which had been the stamping ground of my youth. Accordingly, I selected Newdale, largely because it possessed a very ancient and very comfortable hotel which would serve as a temporary base.

I selected two old and trusted friends, Professor James Wheeler (Mathematics) and Doctor Roger Vaughan (Biochemistry), as my aides-de-camp. Together we moved into the Newdale Hotel and issued regal instructions to the multitude of servants, civil and otherwise, that had been placed at our disposal.

Let there be chemi-labs, physics labs, lecture theatres, high-voltage generators and much apparatus, we commanded. And lo, an army of workmen moved into Newdale and began throwing up prefabricated buildings on ten acres of chosen ground. Let there be physicists, chemists, biophysicists, biochemists, metallurgists, biologists, etc., we said. And the Department of Scientific and Industrial Research began to scour the country for us like an old-time press gang in search of unsuspecting sailors.

In six months the labs were ready and we had more first class scientific personnel than we could possibly use. We also had on our tails what began to look like the entire operational staff of the British Secret Service. At first, I was rather amused by their melodramatic activities. But when someone with a long-range telescopic rifle appeared to think that I would be much improved by death, I at least began to take a kindlier view of the cloak and dagger brigade.

Of course, we had now reached the embarrassing stage where everything was provided and there was nothing else to do but get on with the job.

Required: one Doomsday weapon capable of ironing out the whole human race. It was a tall order, but then I thought I had a rather tall solution. Oddly enough, several of my junior scientists were quite enthusiastic about the project. They came up with such wild schemes as indestructable viruses, radio-activity saturation devices, even anti-gravity fields large enough to drain the planet of its atmosphere and so choke us all to death. I dismissed the more original and enthusiastic members of my team. Such people seemed to me to be rather dangerous.

Besides, although I could countenance people working on the Doomsday project for financial reward and social distinction—as I myself was doing—the thought of somebody developing the weapon because it was the one thing they really wanted to do was somewhat abhorrent. Also, by this time I had an idea of my own. It was elegantly simple. But, above all, its successful development would demand tremendous patience and absolute loyalty.

Having, at the end of the first year, reduced my team to the sort of people one can count on till the death, I outlined to them my own unorthodox idea for an uninhibited thermonuclear furnace that, once the reaction started, would go on consuming matter until the Earth was no more than a wisp of cosmic smoke. After all, on this line of development, the basic problem was merely a matter of temperature. All we had to do was work out a system of matching the internal heat of the sun and then hold it long enough to develop a continuous reaction. Then we could metaphorically sit back while the Earth fried prior to vaporising.

Naturally, my team was utterly appalled by the idea. So was I. And, therefore, in a spirit of grim resolution we settled down to the long process of theoretical exploration, limited extrapolation and fractional experiment that would ultimately provide the logical design of the Doomsday machine.

It took us two years. During that time, I had to make frequent progress reports to the government. Time and again I tried to explain the theory of the Doomsday machine to them in relatively simple terms. But they didn't seem to understand it very clearly. And they seemed to be worried even more by the prospect of success than by the prospect of failure. Also they were hardly comforted by the knowledge that both the Americans and the Russians were now indulging in a Doomsday race themselves.

But I had my own troubles to think about. I was hardly popular with the Great British Public which — whatever one may say or think about it from time to time — usually has the enviable faculty of being fairly sensible in the last resort. Although there was a blanket of secrecy over the details of the Doomsday project, there was no secrecy about its nature. And I was certainly on the short list for being the most disliked man in Britain.

However, assassination and kidnapping are not the kind of activities that appeal to indignant mothers in Croydon or elderly colonels in Cheltenham, so the half-hearted attempts with which I was occasionaly plagued must be ascribed to the *joie de vivre* of certain interested and definitely foreign bodies.

It was in the autumn of 1963 that I felt the time was ripe to make my final report to the Prime Minister, particularly so since the news had then been unofficially leaked that the Russians had their own Doomsday weapon completed. I would have preferred to wait a little longer before announcing that the British device was now operational. But actually there was little more that either I or my team could do. The great thing about a Doomsday device is that you can't try it out experimentally. It is, essentially, a one-shot instrument – and the first shot is the last for all concerned.

A month after the announcement that the British model was triggered and ready to go, the Americans, not be outdone, let it be known that they had completed two quite independent Doomsday machines, presumably, in case one of them failed to work.

Everybody, I imagine, knows the rest of the story. Now that Britain, America and Russia each had their own means of ensuring global destruction, stalemate had been reached once more. But it was a stalemate with a difference.

The great thing about the Doomsday weapon — any Doomsday weapon — was that it rendered war obsolete. Even the generals could see that. After all, there isn't much point in launching a couple of hundred hydrogen warheads against your enemy when all he has to do is to press a button and take you with him.

The military men of both East and West were pretty angry about the whole situation. For it followed that, if war was obsolete, so also were thermonuclear weapons and — ultimately — generals.

And such proved to be the case. In the spring of 1964, after much dithering by all concerned, a summit meeting was arranged in the then international city of Berlin, later to become the first world capital. The President, the Prime Minister and the irrepressible First Secretary of the Communist Party of the Soviet Union made a lot of speeches full of abstract nouns — like justice, freedom, truth, emancipation and equality — and in effect ran through the whole gamut of diplomacy from A to B. But when they had finished playing to the global gallery, they finally got down to business and faced the facts.

And the facts were that atomic weapons were not only out, they were laughable, except as an elaborate means of committing suicide by letting one or two off on your enemy. It was an historic occasion, for it marked the beginning of the first genuine disarmament conference.

By autumn of 1964, Russian inspection teams were busy touring British and American installations throughout the world, observing the dismantling of all military missiles and atomic warheads; while British and American inspection teams were doing the same thing in Russia and the satellite states. The mood became almost hilarious. Everybody was busy swapping military secrets and having a good laugh about how they had devoted the best part of their energies and industries to trying to frighten each other for so long.

But, while the rest of the world was beginning to relax, I and my colleagues were plunged in gloom. We could already see what was coming next.

Sure enough, in January of 1965, some idiot statesman who shall be nameless suggested that, in view of the continued and necessary existence of the Doomsday machines as an insurance against war, it would be safer if each device was manned by a team drawn from the three 'Doomsday Powers'. His proposals boiled down to this: that there should be one senior American officer, one senior Russian officer and one senior British officer at each Doomsday base. The machines would be so rigged that each of the officers would have a key to fit a circuit lock in the control system, and unless all three keys were fitted and turned simultaneously in the locks, it would be impossible to begin even the first stage of programming.

After some preliminary argument, the proposal was

accepted internationally; and this, of course, involved a conference between the various Doomsday scientists. And in the end that would involve what may be adequately described as a few scientific revelations. I was not looking forward to it at all.

But, despite some half-hearted evasive action, by mid-February I found myself in Geneva, closeted one cold, wet evening with Comrade Professor Fyodor Norov, the scientist in charge of the Russian installation, and Dr. George C. Wynkel, director of both American projects.

Fortunately Norov spoke excellent if unorthodox English. But although he and Wynkel seemed very friendly — a little too friendly for my peace of mind — there was a peculiar atmosphere of despondency which none of us seemed able to dispel.

After half an hour of entirely trivial conversation, we had made not the slightest progress towards discussing the problem of Doomsday control, and I seemed to get the impression that we were each taking elaborate care not to be the first to mention the infernal topic. I also had the impression that we were staring quite a lot at each other on a sort of alternating cat-and-mouse basis. I felt distinctly uneasy.

At length, Norov shrugged and said: "This is not good, comrades. We need an ice-breaker, no?" He reached for the telephone and ordered a bottle of vodka.

"Make mine whisky," said Wynkel. "Scotch."

"I'll take whisky, too," I said. "Irish."

Norov ordered a bottle of each.

And then we went on making polite conversation.

It was not until my third double — we were carefully matching each other, glass for glass — that I found enough courage to work slowly round to my big confession.

"Doomsday gadgets that bring universal peace frighten me," I remarked tentatively. "They symbolise the ultimate absurdity of logic. There must be a flaw somewhere."

"No flaw," protested Norov. "But me, I am frightened, too. What about accidents?"

Wynkel laughed. "Be careful," he warned drily, "the accident you have may be your own."

"It's not the theory that worries me," I went on, "it's the practice. The argument for Doomsday weapons is sound enough — they have already brought nuclear disarmament — but, to tell the truth, I could never work up any enthusiasm for having them around."

"Not nice," agreed Norov. "Moreover, damn big pain in the ear."

"Neck," corrected Wynkel.

"To tell the truth," I burst out desperately, "*my* Doomsday machine doesn't work. Long ago we — that is, everyone in the final project team — decided that science was being pulled into politics just a shade too deep. So we made up our minds to only go through the Doomsday motions, so to speak. After all, we didn't want to run the risk of some idiot actually pressing the button."

There was a painful pause.

"That," said Comrade Professor Norov, "was criminal deception." Thoughtfully he poured himself another shot of vodka.

"Hardly British, old boy," remarked Dr. Wynkel. He seemed to be amused. "How did you fool the politicos?"

"We rigged up a thick glass dome on top of a steel tower and fooled about with enough heavy-duty cable to supply all Asia with electricity. And then we just blinded them with science." I grinned ruefully. "It's odd how eager people are to believe that if you just press a button the world will go up in smoke. It's probably something to do with the death wish."

"Or vice versa," suggested Wynkel obscurely. He took a deep breath then said: "The President knew, of course. We felt we had to tell somebody."

"About ours?" I was dumbfounded.

"No," said Wynkel softly. "About ours. Incidentally, *we* went to the trouble of finding out that Doomsday machines just can't be built."

"But, comrade, *we* built one," exclaimed Norov with a gleam in his eye.

"Will it work?" demanded Wynkel calmly.

Norov laughed. "If anybody — how do you say — prod the button, he will make the biggest hole there ever was in Siberia, by damn!" We all looked at each other. Slowly we filled our glasses and raised them.

"To peace," I said.

"Sanity among the nations," added Norov somewhat pompously.

"And scientific moonshine," added Wynkel.

I began to feel ridiculously happy. "Do you think we have any chance of keeping the secret now?"

"Why not?" said Wynkel blandly. "We'll have to pick the international inspection teams carefully, that's all."

"Anyone who talks nonsense," announced Norov with a meaning look, "will be required to take the psychiatric treatment, yes?"

"Yes indeed," said Wynkel. "He sure will."

Well, there you have it — the real Doomsday story. It is now August 31st, 1965, the world is peaceful and virtually disarmed, problems are talked out at the conference table instead of being drowned in a rattle of rockets, and I have just finished my last day as Senior British Doomsday Inspector. My successor is Professor James Wheeler, who has been second-in-command on the project ever since it began. He has an excellent capacity for keeping his mouth shut and his face solemn.

Not, I think, that it would matter much if the truth were published now. People have been chastened by the threat of universal destruction for so long that they would probably regard the truth as a joke in very bad taste.

You know, I think I've earned my knighthood! Norov, of course, is a Hero of the Soviet Union, First Class; and Dr. Wynkel, well, he has already been asked to run for Vice-President next time round.

Tomorrow's Gift

Tomorrow's gift of joy or pain
renews the problem of desire.
Behind each vacant pair of eyes
lurks the sad prisoner of fire.

Anonymous Elizabethan Poet

FROM THE TWENTY-SEVENTH storey of the Central Administrative Building, the city looked like an enormous target, or a complex geometrical amoeba whose nucleus combined the functions of stomach, heart and brain.

Within this duodenal cerebrum were the Co-ordinators, the architects of Nova Mancunia, the self-appointed masters of its fate. Their circular colony was exactly one mile in diameter; for though there were no more than fifty Co-ordinators to the total population of fifty thousand, they were careful to emphasise the privileges of rank.

Each Co-ordinator lived according to his taste. Pre-Elizabethan farmhouses mingled with late Windsor mansions. A Norman church — rebuilt stone by stone, with the obvious addition of central heating and a swimming pool styled as a South Sea lagoon — lay facing an opaque windmill whose sails actually revolved. The most striking residence, perhaps, was that of the Director. He chose to live in a replica of a nineteenth-century mill chimney, which perpetually belched forth a harmless synthetic smoke.

The Central Administrative Building, the only functional element in the whole area, was no more than a hundred feet square and five hundred feet high. It was built entirely of hiduminium and plastic. Surrounding the entire digestive brain-centre of the city was a green belt, also a mile wide. It was a natural park where herds of deer appreciated, by simple analogy, the concept of a finite universe.

Beyond this again lay the mile-wide band which was the domain of five hundred Technicians. Their accommodation was less ambitious than that of the Co-ordinators and occupied less space. They lived in four different types of houses, according to their status. There was the semi-detached cottage, the cottage, the cottage-residence and the residence. Alpha Technicians, only, enjoyed the luxury of a residence and its indoor swimming pool. There were, altogether, fifty residences.

Exactly ninety-five per cent of the Technicians' belt was occupied by electronic factories, power units and a hydroponics plant that, by itself, accounted for one thousand acres. The hydroponics installation, subdivided for convenience into five separate groups, produced Nova Mancunia's entire food supply — from yeast to yams, from apples to apricots, from milk substitute to synthetic mutton.

With the Technicians' belt, the vital region of the city ended. Outside it, there was another green belt and then the Prefrontals' Reservation, the territory reserved for numerous failed human beings. It was the home of men and women who were not Illiterates but who were maladjusted. Some of them had been, potentially or actually, Alpha Technicians, even Alpha Co-ordinators. But they had become, for various reasons, unhappy. Partial readjustment was comparatively simple. Even the old pre-atomic surgeons were able to perform the operation of prefrontal leucotomy. A few brain fibres to be severed, the removal of a small amount of cerebral garbage — anxiety, doubt, resentment, despair — and then there was nothing to worry about. Except that the patient was automatically sentenced to a life of happy retirement, his services being no longer required.

Beyond the Prefrontals' Reservation was the epidermis of Nova Mancunia, the final layer of skin, the mass of the people. They lived in twenty-five glass and concrete hives, each containing one thousand flats. They lived and procreated and died; their enormous blocks of flats being, equally, fertility symbols and tombstones.

Not being Co-ordinators, or Technicians, or Prefrontals they were classified as Illiterates. Some of them were craftsmen or painters; some wrote imaginative histories or old-fashioned poems; some worked the land and produced unhygienic, unnecessary food; some designed clothes that would eventually wear out; and enough of them committed suicide to relieve the Co-ordinators of the problem of an expanding population.

Encircling this outer ring of hives was the wilderness, spotted here and there with other concentric cities; spotted also with round lakes whose water would never drain away through their beds of glass and diamond. These were the monuments of the old Hydrogen Wars.

Six miles to the north was Lake Manchester. It had been one of the first cities to die.

Dr. Krypton gazed through his office window on the twenty-seventh storey of C.A.B. and watched the sails of the Deputy Director's glass windmill go round. It was his business to look for obscure meanings, and he wondered for the hundredth time if there was one here. Perhaps it was the Deputy Director's method of subtly announcing his deviationist tendencies. Certainly, the sails described a revolution, impelled by a material force. Certainly, the law governing the revolution had its sociological parallel . . . But would the Deputy Director be so subtle? Would he, also, with a tested Happiness Quotient of a hundred and fifty, and an Intelligence Quotient of a hundred and eighty, seek to change the status quo? Dr. Krypton dismissed these idle speculations with a shrug, and turned to face the man in the room.

He was a young man, under thirty; more than seventy years younger than the Alpha psychiatrist who now confronted him.

He wore an air of aggressive resentment. But practically all Dr. Krypton's visitors did. It was either that or injured innocence.

What was the man's name? All Dr. Krypton could remember was that it was one he should have remembered. He glanced at the passport in his hands. *Byron, Mark Antony: Ph.D. Elec.: Technician Beta: H.Q. 105, I.Q 115: D.O.B. 2473: Male.*

That was all the information. It was all that need be known. It was more than enough to distinguish Byron, Mark Antony from Byron, Caesar Augustus — if there was one. For it was the story of a life.

"Why has your passport reached my office?" asked Dr. Krypton suddenly.

For a moment, the young man's expression was blank, then he jerked out an answer: "I don't know, sir. I was about to ask you the same question."

It was the usual reaction. Dr. Krypton studied his patient objectively, wondering whether he would be likely to bore or entertain. A recommendation for immediate prefrontal would take care of the first possibility, and an observation visa would provide for the latter.

"You know who I am, of course?" asked the psychiatrist briskly.

"Yes, sir. Co-ordinator Alpha, consultant psychiatrist and neurosurgeon."

"You are aware of my H.Q./I.Q.?"

"One three five, and one seventy."

"Good, we shall perhaps save time. I have the advantage, I see, of fifty-five intelligence points. I have also the ultimate privilege of deciding your fate."

"I understand."

"I hope so. You, on the other hand, theoretically retain the choice of working with or against me. If you feel able to lie successfully, do so by all means. It will be a game of chess, which you will play without a queen."

Dr. Byron appeared to pull himself together. He gazed at the psychiatrist coolly. "I presume my passport was sent to you because my efficiency is questioned?"

Dr Krypton shook his head. "Reasons are never given. While I hold your passport, you are my patient. You will provide the reasons."

"I could suggest a conspiracy."

"That would be tedious. Everyone does — even, on occasion, Co-ordinators Alpha. Fear temporarily decreases intelligence by upwards of twenty per cent."

"Suppose I have no fear?"

Dr. Krypton sighed. "When a man no longer has fear, he is acutely unhappy. I invariably recommend prefrontal."

Dr. Byron seemed suddenly to relax. He smiled. "As I am no longer afraid, I accept both your diagnosis and treatment, sir. When may I expect the operation?"

The psychiatrist became interested. Here, at least, was an unusual approach. Many of those whose passports reached Dr. Krypton anticipated his recommendation and prepared for it in various ways — some by opening an artery, and some by getting drunk. But here was one who seemed willing to short-circuit the entire analysis.

"You are in a hurry," observed Dr. Krypton. "Why do you want your present personality to die?"

The younger man appeared to restrain himself from laughing. "Isn't it already dead?"

"Demonstrably not."

"Then there is no time to lose. In the interests of communal stability, you should amputate it as soon as possible."

"Why?"

"Because," said Dr. Byron calmly, "it generates delusions."

"Perhaps there is no future for anyone without them," suggested Krypton in a dry voice.

Dr. Byron raised his eyebrows. "Do you say that officially?"

It was the psychiatrist's turn to laugh. "Heresy has been permitted for the *elite* ever since the Christian Church began the fashion. Officially, I may find it necessary to become *advocatus diaboli* and express whatever opinions I wish."

Byron was silent for a moment. Then he spoke at great speed. "In the Country of the Blind, the one-eyed man is merely a psychotic. I am a psychotic, Dr. Krypton, because I do not share the reality of blindness. I am obsessed by the delusion of sight. I can see nothing but a slow disintegration in this stupid system of— of caste. On a planet that once supported three thousand million human beings there are now only ten million. They live in a couple of hundred hygienic Nova Mancunias. They do not procreate: they merely reproduce. I have discovered that there is a subtle difference. Has it occurred to you that in the last hundred years History had stopped? Nothing happens any more; nothing is lost, and nothing is gained. All the Nova Mancunias everywhere are as dead and sterile as the lakes of the Hydrogen Wars. They are toy civilisations slowly running down. And there is no one to wind them up."

"Except you," said Krypton with sarcasm. "Why didn't you find a Technician Beta Female, marry her, and sublimate these quixotic notions in an orderly domestic rhythm?"

"The classification of Technician Beta Female supersedes that of Woman," returned Byron. "In any case, I have not found that any variation on the theme of mating is a permanent cure for ideals."

"What do you define as 'ideals'?"

"Irrelevancies," said Byron, "such as truth, love, beauty. And humanity."

"The first three are nonsensical abstractions. The last is a collective noun. No one has agreed on the meanings of any of them, yet they have caused more destruction than the Hydrogen Wars. That is why, in our city-states, we have sacrificed 'ideals' on the altar of stability."

"Assuming that it is better to be a happy pig than an unhappy Socrates?" demanded Byron.

Dr. Krypton shrugged. "Pigs — lamentably now extinct — never had a reasonable Happiness Quotient. At best, they experienced contentment. Socrates, on the other hand, enjoyed himself hugely, if the old accounts are to be believed."

"But happiness consists in adjusting one's self to the world. I do not think — "

"On the contrary, you *do* think, Dr. Byron, but not expertly. Otherwise you would see that contentment is obtained by adjusting oneself to the world, a proposition supported by the extinct pig, which was a creature adequately conditioned to its environment. Conversely, Socrates preferred to adjust the world to himself— and derived the greatest happiness. As you know, he died tranquilly, which is to say happily. Death, for him, was the final luxury. He was fulfilled."

Dr. Byron looked perplexed. "Perhaps a prefrontal will turn me into a happy Socrates," he said with irony.

Krypton smiled. "Or it may save you from being an unhappy pig. Here is your passport. You will need it because tonight you will visit Illiterates Block Seven, where the girl Thalia doubtless awaits you. One is reluctant to believe that all philosophy derives from sex, but the confirmation is provided daily."

For the first time, Byron displayed fear. "What do you know about Thalia?"

"My dear fellow, I warned you that you would have to play without a queen. You came to me yesterday, also, and I gave you deep hypnosis. Believe me, it is less tiring for all concerned. Not only did you tell me all about this Thalia, but you described her charms so minutely that I would have no difficulty in recognising her in the flesh, so to speak. She is twenty-three and affects subjective painting. Her H.Q. is about twenty points higher than yours, and her I.Q. about twenty-five lower. Her father was a Technician Alpha Prefrontal, and her mother an Illiterate. She is volatile and resilient. Need I say more?"

"What are you going to do about her?" Byron could not keep the anxiety from his voice.

"I am a psychiatrist not an inquisitor. She is an Illiterate, therefore I need take no action."

The younger man was genuinely puzzled. "Why, then, are you allowing me to see her again?"

"I should have thought that was self-evident. By leaving you free to visit her, I weaken your resistance. If you take advantage of this final opportunity, you will be emotionally exhausted when you come to me tomorrow. If you do not see her, you will be frustrated by an unresolved conflict. Either is advantageous, for I shall have to decide what to do with you tomorrow. It will be useful to observe you under stress."

"Why do you tell me this?"

"I can afford to have no secrets. Good morning, Dr. Byron. Here, you are forgetting your passport!"

"Will he give you a prefrontal?" she asked quietly.

They were walking hand in hand through the few acres of carefully designed woodland between Block Seven and Block Eight. Lights, shining from the uncurtained windows of flats, appeared to dance between the leaves of birch, oak and sycamore. Here and there, in symmetrical grassy hollows, Illiterates Male lay with Illiterates Female, transforming the mechanics of coition into an old subjective mystery.

"I expect so," he answered. "There is no other solution."

"We could run away," she said. "We could try to reach the Primitives in the Highlands. They say there are several thousand of them north of the Grampians."

He shook his head. "The Co-ordinators would allow an Illiterate to escape, but not a Technician. Besides, we can't even be sure that the Primitives exist."

"Are you afraid?" asked Thalia.

"Yes, for both of us. It will be better when I am sent to the Reservation. Then we shall be able to meet frequently."

She gripped his hand tightly. "After the operation, you may not love me any more."

"You can teach me, all over again."

"I . . . I may not want to. You'll feel different about things. With the Prefrontals, nothing matters deeply. You'll get bored, and make love to some Prefrontal woman, and won't be able to understand how—how I feel about it."

He stopped, put his arm round her and whispered: "Look at the stars. They're the memory patterns of the cosmos. They are patterns of inconceivable purpose on the brain of space. To them, Nova Mancunia is nothing. It is not even the characteristic of a diseased astro-spore. The constellations are outside our time. They shone with the same brilliance when Lake Manchester was a teeming city: they will continue to shine when Nova Mancunia is a more doubtful legend than Troy."

"I'm not sure I understand," she said slowly. "But when you talk like that I want to believe without understanding."

"Do the stars," he asked, "seem still and tranquil?"

"When we look at them together," she answered, "I begin to think we might borrow their stillness."

She heard him laugh softly. "They are hurtling by at millions of kilometres an hour," he said. "They are burning themselves to death to illuminate a journey without destination. They are racing headlong to extinction, or else they are the only still points in a whirlpool of space. Which is it?"

"I don't know."

"Neither do I: and that, my darling, is the greatest secret in the world. Just as they might be dying by the light-year, so we might expand one moment of life into eternity."

Slowly, insistently, he pulled her down — down into the grassy hollow where they stood. Down through a tunnel of darkness to the oldest innocence of all. Presently, in its own compelling ritual, love became a communicable experience of death . . .

There they lay, a Technician Beta Male and an Illiterate Female; each, in a different fashion, awaiting the slow metabolism of resurrection.

Dr. Krypton stared absently through his office window at the Deputy Director's glass windmill. The enigma remained. Some day, perhaps, the sails would cease to turn, and the passport of a Co-ordinator Alpha would lie on the psychiatrist's desk . . .

Revolution or evolution? It seemed to be the peculiar genius of twenty-fifth century man to be an enemy of both.

The psychiatrist heard the door open and said, without turning round: "Good morning, Dr. Byron. If one and a half squirrels ate one and a half nuts in one and a half minutes, how many nuts would nine squirrels eat in nine minutes?"

"Fifty-four," said Byron after a short pause.

"Three seconds," observed Krypton. "You are moderately alert . . . I trust you achieved catharsis last night?"

"I did. I killed her!"

Dr. Krypton turned to face his visitor. "That is interesting. Why did you not kill yourself also?"

"Because I needed to live in order to kill you."

"You are probably stronger than I am," said the psychiatrist calmly. "It appears that Nova Mancunia will presently need a new Co-ordinator Alpha; and neurosurgeons are difficult to replace. Unfortunately, Dr. Byron, you cannot kill the system."

"I can try."

"You can fail. That is all. Now you had better begin your failure by killing me."

Byron moved forward, then suddenly stopped. He moved forward again, then stopped. His whole body was trembling. Beads of sweat broke out on his forehead.

"I am afraid," said the psychiatrist, "that I took advantage of the deep hypnosis to rearrange, temporarily, your pattern of compulsion and taboo. As you see, it was quite justified. If you lay a hand on me, I assure you there will be no resistance. I have considered your case since yesterday. There does not seem to be any alternative to a prefrontal leucotomy—officially."

"And unofficially?" asked Byron, staring at him dully.

"I shall operate on you, Dr. Byron, but I shall merely make an incision, then close it. There will be no severance of brain fibre."

"Why?"

"Because, my dear fellow, the human race needs you. Until that need is manifest, you will live in the Prefrontal Reservation."

"One of us is quite mad," said Byron slowly.

"I am," admitted Krypton. "It is incurable. You see, I too have no faith in Nova Mancunia. The present society is now static, and there will come a time when it will fail. That will be the signal for a return to humanity."

"Did you make me kill her?" demanded Byron abruptly.

"I did. You, perhaps, will need to die before a new society is established. I have merely made it easier for you."

For a minute, Dr. Byron remained silent. When he spoke,

his voice was quiet, his manner calm. "When will you operate?"

"Tomorrow morning."

"Are you really not going to cut the fibre, or is that suggestion part of the treatment?"

Dr. Krypton smiled. "It is an interesting point, because you will never know. Good morning, Dr. Byron."

Presently, Dr. Krypton took his customary place by the window. Outside, the sun was shining, and a slight breeze turned the sails of the glass windmill round and round and round.

The Jar of Latakia

MALLORY LIFTED THE makeshift lid of the tankard and sniffed curiously. It was just an ordinary stoneware tankard, the kind one used to buy full of mustard in pre-war Vienna. There was a crude, dark red bas-relief of St. Nikolaus on the side.

But the tankard did not now contain mustard. A few stiff, dried flakes of what appeared to be tobacco lay at the bottom. It smelled like tobacco and it felt like tobacco, the kind of tobacco that might have been mislaid round about the turn of the century. There seemed to be a little less than half an ounce.

A confirmed pipe-smoker and *soi-disant* connoisseur of tobacco, Mallory fingered the brittle flakes and held them close to his nose for a few moments.

"Latakia," he pronounced audibly and confidently, feeling sure of his verdict.

At that point, there was a knock at the door. Mallory put the Latakia back into the tankard, which he returned to the oven of the disused kitchen range, where he had found it. Then he went to receive his visitor, and promptly forgot all about it.

John Mallory had occupied the country cottage for about a month. The fact that the previous owner — a Colonel Harrys — had hanged himself upon a convenient apple tree in the garden made the purchase of the cottage an easy matter. Mallory had offered a ridiculously low sum which had promptly been accepted.

For Mallory, the attraction of Rone House lay in its isolation. He wanted to get on with his work; and for that he needed solitude. City life might have its merits and consolations for the struggling artist; but for the successful one, as Mallory had found to his cost, it also had its limitations. One was expected to entertain and be entertained. One was expected to scintillate in a miasma of vapid parties. One was expected to be gregarious and eccentric, and to use a studio largely for the cultivation of multiple and complex love affairs.

In such a world, John Mallory was out of character. Thirty-five years old and a bachelor with a reasonable income, he felt just a little vulnerable. And of late, his vulnerability had been tested by one or two aspiring women, single and otherwise. From these and from other distractions, he had fled into the country. Now, at last, he was beginning to get down to solid work again.

The north bedroom of the cottage made a comfortable studio. Mallory did not regret the loss of rustling silk of taffeta and the bright red smiles. At Rone House he met only those human beings it was necessary to meet — chiefly trades-people. He lived alone and liked it.

One morning, shortly after breakfast, he took himself up to the studio to continue work on a rather ambitious portrait. It was the head and shoulders of a woman, the kind of woman John Mallory had never known. He needed no model, and was guided only by the fleeting but profound impressions that his waking mind managed to retain from a persistent though damnably elusive dream.

On this particular morning, he was engaged in the delicate project of painting the eyes. Three times he had scraped the paint off the canvas with his palette knife. The light was good, his working conditions were excellent, but somehow the colours were muddy. Mallory gazed at his untidy palette with distaste. None of the pigments upon it possessed the quality he needed. The blues were dull and lifeless; the greens stodgy and opaque. How then could he hope to achieve the transparent and luminous turquoise that would bring those vacant eyes to a mysterious, independent life?

He puffed furiously at his pipe, concentrating upon the insoluble problem. Presently, he noticed that the pipe was cold. Muttering an irritable curse, he reached for his pouch, recalling as he did so that he had taken the last filling after breakfast. Mallory cursed freely, and stalked grimly downstairs in vain but hopeful search for an odd tin of tobacco.

After five minutes he gave it up, and bestowed eloquent if unreasonable maledictions on the village shop that was nearly two miles away.

It was then that Mallory remembered the jar of Latakia. He went into the kitchen and took it from the old kitchen range. Removing the lid, he stared at the dark, crisp shreds distastefully. "Poisonous stuff!" he muttered to himself. But at that particular point, Mallory was prepared to burn his throat out, if only he was allowed to solve the problem of the eyes.

So he decided to brew a mug of tea as an antidote to the probable effects of smoking that dry and ancient tobacco. Waiting for the kettle to boil, he idly mused upon this first and only relic of Colonel Harrys that remained in the cottage. He began to wonder why the Colonel — from all accounts a stock military type — should choose such a dramatic way of taking his life.

"Probably smoked too much of this damn tobacco," he concluded uncharitably. Then, as steam came from the spout of the kettle, he considered the possibility that the Latakia might have been in Rone House long before Colonel Harrys came.

Back in the studio, Mallory banished all such conjectures from his mind as he contemplated the canvas before him, occasionally sipping tea, and absently stuffing shreds of Latakia into his pipe.

Presently, the fragrance peculiar to such tobacco began to fill the studio, blue skeins of smoke wreathing leisurely across the still atmosphere.

Presently, Mallory found a more promising way of approaching his problem; and then, naturally, simply, inevitably, the means of solving it. He began to work quickly and silently.

Presently, a pair of blue-green, slightly luminous eyes regarded him gravely from the enigmatic canvas.

The girl was sitting in the chair when Mallory awoke. She was staring at him gravely with the same blue-green eyes.

His heart lurched violently, and he glanced with a terrible effort of will at the canvas. Nothing had changed. Here, then, was the original of the painting.

Mallory sat up suddenly on his camp-bed and gaped. The reality of the situation began to penetrate the sleepy mist that still shrouded his returning consciousness. More important than solving the mystery of how he came to be asleep on the camp-bed was this urgent, three-dimensional mystery of the girl.

"In God's name, who are you?" demanded Mallory, his voice sharp with a peculiar fear. He heard his own taut words break the silence, and was startled by their intensity.

The unreasonable surge of fear drowned all rational feeling, swept away all common-sense explanations or possibilities, as Mallory took in the details of her odd dress; the long, divided skirt gleaming like dull metal; the black translucent spider-web of blouse, offset by curious brooches; the broad belt round her waist. And even as the scene burned itself indelibly in his mind, he registered the insignificant fact that the clock had stopped — at twenty past eleven. Therefore he had been asleep for less than five minutes, or more than twenty-four hours.

From the sluggish stupidity of awakening, his thoughts had accelerated to a break-neck speed, so that his mind was busy exploring all possibilities before the girl had answered his question.

Her voice, leisurely and musical, was like a cool sedative to Mallory's high fever of unreason.

"It is natural for you to be afraid," she said. "That is why I wanted you to awaken slowly — to lessen the shock. Please look into my eyes!"

It was neither a request nor a command, yet Mallory instantly acceded or obeyed; he was not sure which.

For a moment, the deep luminosity of her gaze seemed to darken the room, seemed to swallow him; and he felt drawn through opaque, swirling pools of darkness. Then everything was light again. But he no longer felt tense or afraid. Calmly and intelligently he awaited her explanation.

She smiled. "That feels better, doesn't it?"

He nodded. "Who are you?" he asked once again. But the terror had left his voice.

"First let me prepare you," she said in the odd, leisurely tone. "It would be better, I think, if you could accept this experience as a rather vivid dream, nothing more. You see, your mind is not attuned to face this particular actuality without suffering a great stress. Can you believe that you are dreaming?"

Once more he met the compelling darkness of her eyes. "If you think it is necessary," he said calmly, "I will believe that I am dreaming." He turned towards the canvas. "But as you see, the dream has not entirely taken me by surprise."

She followed his glance, and her smile became almost mischievous. "Naturally, there would be a certain amount of subconscious preparation," she explained. "Your — your submerged self would anticipate this experience long before your conscious self was able to enter it."

Mallory, already accepting the dream-like quality of the situation, was beginning to react almost naturally.

"I'm not sure that I believe in predestination," he remarked with a thinly-disguised scepticism. "Or even in clairvoyance."

She seemed to be amused. "You won't deny that there is a certain relation between cause and effect?"

Her amusement was infectious. After all, thought Mallory, if this is a dream, then I'll have a damn good two-pennyworth. And if it isn't a dream, it's certainly diverting.

He shook his head in answer to her question. "Nevertheless, I do assert that there is such a thing as Free Will."

As if by chance, her gaze rested on Mallory's pipe, which lay on the floor. He noticed it — and remembered the Latakia — for the first time.

"Did that have anything to do with it?" he asked quickly.

The girl's eyes were laughing. "Perhaps," she said non-committally.

Mallory felt he was making a fool of himself.

Then suddenly she became serious. "The first thing you must accept," she said, "is that we exist in different kinds of time." She paused to let the full meaning of her words sink in.

There was a few seconds' silence, during which Mallory became unaccountably cold. He stared at her, trying to comprehend the strange transition from a normal studio session to a tightrope walk between daydream and nightmare.

"You mean," he said hoarsely, "you belong to the past?"

For a moment, the girl looked surprised. Then the latent power in her eyes seemed to reach out and hold him.

"No, Mr. Mallory," she said quietly. "But I'm afraid you do!" He began to smile again. "You see," she added gently, yet with a curious compulsion, "I happen to know that you died nearly a hundred years ago!"

Looking out of the window, Mallory knew beyond doubt

that what she had said was true.

Until twenty past eleven — or, more accurately, until he had fallen asleep — the view from the studio window had been a panorama of woodland. This was now replaced by the runway of a vast airfield; and in the distance was a cluster of strange, shiny hemispheres which — so the girl told him — were hangars. Mallory was inclined to believe her, especially as a huge aircraft, a slender wingless fuselage, had just passed overhead with terrifying silence.

There were beads of moisture on his forehead, but his hands were ominously cold. It became vitally necessary to keep on talking: a pathetic attempt to assert his own existence. The girl standing by his side watched him with a curious, intimate detachment.

"But this is all nonsense!" he exploded. "It just isn't so! It's some kind of delusion I — I — "

"It is so," she asserted simply, with a hint of compassion in her voice. "But for you, I agree, it is nonsense. It is outside your terms of reference, just as your own world is beyond my experience."

"Look here," said Mallory harshly, "how the devil do you fit into this bloody nightmare?"

The girl studied his tense expression, trying to will him into a calmer state of mind. "I've already told you," she said patiently. "I am what you would call, I think, a psychiatric worker. It is my business to study certain peculiar experiences which, in your day, were supposed to be simple hallucinations."

"And I," said Mallory sardonically, "am therefore one of your guinea pigs."

"Exactly. We have reason to believe that Time, or History, or Experience — call it what you will — is playing some rather strange tricks in this cottage. I am, so to speak, investigating the reputed hauntings." She smiled suddenly. "May I say that I find you a very interesting and human sort of ghost."

Mallory was not deceived by the lightness of her tone. "There have been others?" he asked quickly.

She nodded. "One, at least. Perhaps more. You see, we were only able to localise the disturbances shortly before the appearance of our last visitor."

Mallory took a leap in the dark: "Colonel Harrys?"

"Did you know him?" countered the girl quickly.

Mallory gave a bitter laugh. "He hanged himself. That's how I came to get the cottage."

"We know all about his death," she said. "Poor man, he was unable to stand the shock. You, on the other hand, are taking it much better."

"Which just goes to show that psychiatry hasn't advanced a great deal," he remarked drily.

"Possibly not, but telepathy has. You must remember, Mr. Mallory, that unless you choose to shut me out, I can witness most of your thoughts."

Mallory stared at her. Then a slight smile played about his lips.

"It's no use trying to shock me," she said imperturbably, "It is perfectly natural of you to think of me as a woman, and to use your imagination to satisfy your curiosity. I accept the compliment in the spirit in which it is given."

He detected a slight glitter in her eyes, and was suddenly pleased. "People must be pretty uninhibited in this brave new world," he remarked with a thin smile.

"They need to be," said the girl evenly.

The clock was still at eleven twenty; the portrait was still on the easel; the airfield was still visible through the window and the girl had not yet disappeared.

Mallory had recovered himself sufficiently to offer some tea to her — the pot he had brewed was still extraordinarily hot — and he went down to the kitchen for an extra cup and saucer. There he discovered the kettle still puffing steam through its spout, though he remembered turning the gas out before, as he noted grimly, he had turned into a ghost. He began to have his own idea of the kind of dimension in which he now found himself.

On his return to the studio, he watched the girl sip her cup of tea with intense curiosity. He was disappointed. Nothing happened.

"Tell me," he said suddenly, "did I fall, or was I pushed?"

The girl regarded him thoughtfully. "I imagine you pushed yourself, Mr. Mallory. We — of the present time, or your future — certainly had no hand in it, if that is what you think."

Mallory was silent for a moment or two. Then he said: "I expect Colonel Harrys was a pipe-smoker, too."

The girl chose to appear puzzled. "Does that have any bearing?" Then she added: "I see you are thinking about some peculiar tobacco you have smoked."

Mallory laughed. "A jar of Latakia. A few harmless shreds of Latakia. A Viennese mustard-pot stuffed away idly in an old kitchen range. You people of the future seem to be good at riddles — what do you make of that?"

"You want me to say that it has strange properties," she answered quietly. "That, in fact, it is responsible for projecting you a hundred years forward. But I don't know, and neither, I think, do you."

"Oh, yes *I* do," said Mallory. "I know damn well! But it's good to find that the inhabitants of this brave new world are not omniscient, after all. There are more things, Horatio, than are dreamt of in your telepathy." He began to laugh at his own misquotation. He began to laugh raucously and loudly.

She slapped his face. The laughter stopped suddenly. Mallory stared vacantly through the window. "Thank you," he said in an unsteady voice. "I'm sorry."

"You began your painting before you touched this

Latakia," she said abruptly. "How did you come to paint my portrait?"

"It came in a dream," said Mallory in a toneless murmur. "It came in a dream, and I was haunted by the eyes of someone I would never know. Now, I have met you, and it is different. Because one cannot love the future: one can only be afraid, damnably afraid. Or mad. When did I die?"

For a moment, the girl was off-guard. His sudden glance caught the brief pity in her eyes.

"At the end of your life", she replied softly. "And that is when each of us dies, at the end of our life."

"The year," insisted Mallory. "What year? You said you knew!"

"I do know, but it is not good that I should tell you. Besides, I do not know the year in which you left your own world."

"Nineteen fifty-six," he said quickly. "What year did I die?"

The girl did not meet his gaze. For the first time she seemed unsure of herself. "Nineteen eighty-eight," she said hesitantly. "I am as foolish to tell you as you are to ask."

"Liar," said Mallory cheerfully. "It's comforting to know that women haven't learned to lie any better. You might have fooled Harrys, but not me. I have painted your eyes."

"And what did you see there?"

"The truth!"

"What is the truth?"

"Ask Jesting Pilate," taunted Mallory.

"It is time you went back," she said quickly.

Mallory pointed to the clock. "I have abolished time. Time will stand still until I'm ready for it."

"It is dangerous to stay."

"I accept the danger," he said recklessly. "I have conquered time to find my ideal woman; and now I am told to go back. Your attitude, my dear, is essentially feminine. You should never have tempted a homeless ghost."

His vision was becoming blurred, but he could still see

clearly her eyes. They spoke to him silently from a great distance. In them he recognised the truth of his own careless words. But already it was too late.

"What is your name?" he demanded, standing still and swaying like a drunken man. "Whose name shall I call when the stars are dark? Whose portrait shall I gaze at in this empty room?"

Now the room itself was fading. He could no longer see her. Yet, when she spoke, her voice was low and close.

"I am Ann," she whispered, "and you are John. Don't you see, we can't be ourselves because we are separated by time! You must go back! You must enter your own world again."

"Ann, where are you? I can't see any more! Give me your hand!"

She gave him her hand, hoping to lead him to the camp-bed and force him to relax. But with a sudden, surprising vigour, Mallory took her in his arms, blindly seeking her lips.

The darkness became a whirlpool, and slowly the whirlpool grew into a sea of silence.

The hammer crashed again and again, relentlessly. Mallory opened his eyes slowly, very slowly. He looked towards the sound of the hammer. The clock fingers pointed to twenty past eleven. The hammer blows subsided into a steady, even ticking.

Mallory looked about him in bewilderment and fear, half expecting the room, with all its maddening stillness, to dissolve into yet another timeless dream. But the room remained, quiet and eloquent, mute with secrets. The only evidence of that strange interlude was the extra cup and saucer, lying by the chair.

The cup was still warm, still bearing the imprint, thought Mallory bitterly, of those elusive lips.

He heard an echo of that voice, the soft, low voice that was a hundred years away . . . *"I am Ann, and you are John. Don't you see, we can't be ourselves because we are separated by time! You must go back . . .*"

"Blast it, I've come back!" he shouted hopelessly. "Back to a quiet dose of madness!"

Suddenly his gaze fell on the canvas. The blue-green, slightly luminous eyes met his own in a level vacant stare. The lips were immobile, silent; and he knew that he would never hear them speak again, unless . . .

"Hell and damnation!" he sobbed, fighting the urge to shake and crush the canvas in an insane effort to force it into becoming the living woman.

Mallory fled from the room, afraid of doing violence to all that was left of his dream.

Down in the kitchen, his trembling fingers held the jar of Latakia. There were, perhaps, three fillings left. His first impulse was to hurl the jar and its contents through the window: his second impulse was to preserve it carefully, against the time when he would recover the necessary courage to recreate, in his studio, the conditions for — madness.

Mallory shuddered, and replaced the tobacco in its accustomed hiding-place. There were beads of moisture on his forehead; for he knew now that his will was broken, and knew also that he could never enter that room again.

Two days later, haggard, unshaven, sleepless, he came to what appeared to be the only reasonable decision. Having made it, Mallory felt curiously free.

There remained but one or two letters to write. When they were finished, he went briskly about the task of hunting up a piece of old rubber piping he remembered seeing somewhere. Having found it, he made his way to the garage. He smiled grimly to himself, knowing that Colonel Harrys, at least, would have understood.

Later, the Coroner and other interested persons would doubtless dwell upon the unusual phenomenon of a man committing suicide while calmly smoking his pipe.

Rone House had been empty and quiet for some time; though its reputation was not forgotten, and the executors were unable to sell it even at a ridiculously nominal price. Prospective buyers would suspiciously inspect the attractive country cottage, testing every beam and floorboard, seeking some explanation for the tempting sum at which it was offered. But the occasional prospective tenants would uncover a detailed and startling history (factual and otherwise) over a leisurely tankard at any of the nearby village taverns. Thereafter, as they were warned in slow country dialect, they pursued the matter at their own risk. It was eighteen months before anyone did so.

He was a young man in his early thirties, an impecunious novelist in search of solitude and atmosphere. A pleasant, intelligent young man, sceptical and credulous.

He picked his way up the grassy drive one fine spring morning with the agent's keys in his hands. In sunlight, Rone House looked an attractive proposition. The interior had been thoroughly cleaned and decorated. Even the old kitchen range seemed bright and serviceable.

The young man was not yet to know that in the disused oven there lay a stoneware tankard containing a few dark, brittle shreds. He surveyed the cottage with satisfaction, impulsively deciding that there, if anywhere, was the place to finish his book.

It was a fine, warm day; and the spring optimism was infectious. Oddly enough, the new tenant was a confirmed pipe-smoker.

The Unicorn

THE WORLD WAS a village — a village, a fen, a lake, a river and a few square miles of countryside; tenanted by two or three hundred people; lost in the heart of a green, surprising land.

News was news of the soil, news of the weather, news of an enclosed world. You looked at the faces of the children; you watched their movements against the background they had always known; children of an enclosed world.

Ginny was nine — Reginald Redgrave, son of Reginald Redgrave, son of a man. His father was a saddler. They lived in a house that had been built the year Cromwell's head gazed sightless over London. It didn't mean much. The house was what it always was. The sparrows still squabbled in the thatch, and woodsmoke still curled its simple message to the ageless sky.

In the winter there were the frosty mornings, the pictures in the evening fire, the lamplight in a world of shadows. In summer there was the earth and the sky, and all the unclaimed continents of childhood.

He was nine; and already they were planning his life. They wanted him to become a vet. So they loaded him down with books about animals. He didn't like animals; he didn't dislike them. Soon, with the exception of dragons, brontosauri, pterodactyls and similar fantastic creatures, he began to develop a thinly covered hatred for all that had feathers or four feet.

The dead starlings gave evidence of his prowess with a catapult; the rabbits were thoroughly familiar with his ability to smoke out.

Ginny was a boy, healthy and happy amid the quiet roll of seasons.

In the holidays he would, with considerable industry, taste the keen delight of doing nothing. The horizon was pleasant. Over it were things unknown, unimaginable. The horizon moved with you, carrying its secrets until the time when you would find a way to stride over its edge. The river was green, green with the bigness of an always moving, always waiting monster, coiling among valleys, hurrying its message of death and treasure to the hungry ear of the sea. The sky was a tent, like the tent in a story, large enough for all the armies of the world, small enough to carry in your pocket.

Ginny enjoyed it. He could watch the world through the right or wrong end of a telescope at will.

His favourite retreat was Long House, a broad heap of rubble and broken masonry, of charred and weathered woodwork that lay on a small hill hugging the far side of the lake. Its present condition was the result of a political difference which had been settled, after a fashion, in the time of Charles the Second. The centuries lay heavily upon it. He liked that. There, by incantation, he would conjure the shapes of battles that could never have been.

He did not like to be there with other children. It was always easier to wait until they had gone.

One morning he went there, knowing quite well that something would happen. Something did happen; sufficiently frightening to be beautiful, sufficiently beautiful to be frightening.

It was a morning when the world was still, when the polished mirror of the lake held the trees in statuesque reflection, and the burning light of the sun was a still fire upon its surface. It was a morning when a swallow's wing could be heard, and when the thunder of distant machines rolled across the still music of the shires.

Ginny was sitting among the remains of a fallen colonnade, a late and rather extravagant addition to what had been the original Long House. He was busy stirring up a small ant-hill with a piece of dead birch. Revenge for a couple of ant-bites when he had been rolling lazily on the sandy earth.

Suddenly, against the background of spinney and tall firs, he saw a flash of white — there and gone! A flash of white that should have been merely some unaccountable reflection of sunlight, or the noisy drift of yesterday's picnic wrappings restless in the bushes. A flash of white that should have been something other than what it was, than what Ginny had seen — the noiseless retreat of a tall, stately animal carrying a white flame in the centre of its forehead.

He sat still and listened. No sound. Nothing beyond the leisurely drone of flies and bees, the distant grumbling of a farm tractor, the sound of his own heart.

Hope of battles was forgotten. He had seen what none had seen. Cautiously, he gazed about him. At the ground; through the trees; up at the sky. He strained to listen until, by the high-pitched sound in his ears, he heard his own straining. There was nothing! Only the sky, the trees and the birch stick — and a small, fierce globe of disappointment.

Perhaps the creature had been frightened; perhaps his sudden movement . . . He went back to the ant-hill and stared irresolutely at the stupendous activity by the side of his feet. He sat down and waited, not daring to look towards the spinney but ostensibly watching the ants; though every now and again he gave a swift and guilty glance out of the corners of his eyes.

Time passed. Ginny became conscious of the sun's climb. He watched the shortening movement of shadows across the vast pinpoint of his world. He felt hungry. It must be time to go for the meal that would be waiting. He stayed.

Soon he would have to go. Soon they would come to look for him. Then everything would be over. But he stayed. He stayed and was rewarded for his faith.

Noiselessly, so that, waiting for it as he was, he was quite unaware of its presence until it was within a few yards of him, the unicorn trotted across the ruins and stood still. With all his force, Ginny restrained the jerk of fear and joy that trembled in him. Slowly he turned his face towards the creature. It did not move. It did not disappear. Boy and beast regarded each other.

After a time he stood up. The unicorn started, tossed its head so that the sunlight flashed brilliantly upon its polished horn, but it did not turn away. Arching its beautiful neck, it waited. Ginny walked slowly towards it.

The unicorn breathed heavily through its nostril and pawed the ground, tossing its head so that the sharp horn waved and pointed through the air in a bright, menacing way. Ginny did not stop. *It will kill me*, he thought, feeling a sharp pain in his chest where the horn would pin him to the earth. *It will kill me*. But he went on, stretching out a shaking hand to touch its glossy flank.

Anxiously, he stroked. He could feel the quivering muscles slacken. The white head drooped lazily. To his surprise, Ginny noticed that he had started to breathe again.

He bent down and pulled up a handful of unappetising grass. The unicorn looked at him indulgently and began to nibble the grass. Ginny started to cry quietly.

After a while, by mutual consent, the meeting ended. The unicorn turned to amble off through the fir trees. Ginny prepared to go home and face a scolding mother.

"Tomorrow, I'll come tomorrow," he said.

Clearly, the unicorn understood. No doubt crossed Ginny's mind.

He had been right. It had happened. An extremely personal thing. And *he* had been chosen!

He walked home obliviously. Automatically climbed the stile, automatically jumped from stone to stone across the river. When he was within a few yards of the door, he realised that he would have to say something. He could think of nothing that seemed right.

"I forgot the time," he said. It did not convince anyone, but it was all he could bring himself to say.

The sarcasm was not felt; the cold meal was not tasted. He knew now what he had always suspected — that family, home and village were all only part of some conspiratorial dream. A dream designed to keep him away from reality, from the unicorn. And it had almost succeeded. Almost!

For the rest of the day he was strangely quiet, strangely inactive. He sat by the window, dreamily gazing past the garden fence. Even his father, who had little or no time for the ways of a child, decided that he was sickening for something.

Twilight came; evening. Ginny realised that he would only waken up when he went to sleep. And at last, in that strange undimensional state of mind, he went up to his room. His eyes closed and he saw before him the compelling eyes of the unicorn, brighter than stars, deeper and swifter than the river. They swelled until they were greater than the lake. They became twin, burning suns. They became cold, falling moons.

When morning came he felt very tired. He got up and shook himself. He laid his face in a bowl of cold water until he could hold his breath no longer. Then he went down to breakfast. He was very hungry.

Today, I shall go there again, he thought. A wave of happiness surged through him. He dropped his knife and fork with a clatter, and made for the door. His mother, seeing the look on his face, was unaccountably afraid.

"Ginny!" she called. "Come back and finish your breakfast. You've eaten hardly anything."

"I don't want any more. I've — I've had enough."

She sighed. A sigh of exasperation; adult incomprehension. "Why all the hurry? Where are you going?"

He tried to sound casual. "Out, up by the old house."

"Well, mind the river, then, and don't stay out so long today!"

He made his escape quickly.

Free! He ran along the lane and across the fields. Crossing the river, he slipped from a stone. The water came a little higher than his knees. When he got to the other side he sat down and took his shoes and stockings off. He went on, carrying them in his hand.

It was the same as yesterday; the same kind of day; the same kind of sky; the lake still and burning. He knew it would happen again. *It was bound to!*

He sat down amid the wreckage of the colonnade. There was a ritual to be followed. He looked for the birch stick and began to stir up the ants.

Nothing happened. He must be patient. He put down the stick and tried to resign himself to waiting. Again he found himself following the sun's movement by the contracting shadows. He became absorbed by the prospect of leaves and twigs slowly coming into the sunlight. He recognised the individual contours of pebbles and fragments of stone that he had watched with similar care the day before.

Time passed and nothing happened. He began to be afraid. Perhaps he had done something wrong. Perhaps, in some way, he had offended the unicorn and it had rejected him. He watched the sunlight creeping between the stones and began to be afraid.

In the distance, he heard footsteps — the feet of men. He looked across the lake and saw them tramping over the field, two men carrying guns. His heart started to beat faster.

They might be out shooting rabbits; they might be hoping to get the fox that had finished off half a dozen turkeys; they might be wanting to do any one of a number of reasonable things. But suppose . . . suppose they knew about the unicorn! Suppose they wanted the unicorn . . .

Hastily, he looked round. The unicorn was nowhere to be seen.

But what if he had been watched yesterday? What if they knew that the unicorn would come to meet him? *What if they were using him to trap the unicorn?*

He wanted to run. He wanted to stay, to watch, to make sure.

He gazed across the ruins of Long House towards the little hillock that had once been part of an ornamental garden. It was big enough to hide behind. He could stay behind there, and if he could not watch what was going on, at least he could hear.

Perhaps, if the unicorn did come, he would have time to frighten it away. Or perhaps he would be able to attract their attention and give the unicorn a chance.

He scrambled across to the hillock, ran round the other side and flattened himself against the slope. His ears were strained to catch every sound. Now and again he turned his head anxiously glancing towards the fir trees. There was nothing to be seen. Perhaps, after all, this was why the unicorn had not come. Perhaps it had known there would be a trap.

He heard the voices of the men. They were coming nearer. He buried his hands in the loose soil of the hillock, as if it were about to move suddenly and he must hold on. He clenched the earth tightly in his hands, twisting with his knuckles as if to work deeper. His forehead was warm and sticky. Beads of moisture fell into his eyes.

Soon he could hear what they were saying.

"That white devil! I've just about had enough. It's the worst there's been in these parts for a long time."

"Far and away," agreed the other voice. "A real rogue, and

sly as they come. It took five from George's place last week — two in broad daylight! If we don't get it soon . . ."

Behind the hillock, the terrible anguish of a small boy exploded silently. Blood trickled from the palm of a hand in which finger nails had buried themselves. The blood welled slowly, mingling with dry earth.

"I've seen it round here two or three times, but I didn't have a gun . . . It's a fly creature, that one — fast as light."

They sat down and smoked, resting their guns across their knees, oblivious of so much, yet alert for what they sought.

The minutes passed. Behind the hillock, the boy felt himself unable to move. Anxiously, painfully he strained his eyes towards the tree.

Suddenly, he saw it; saw a small, indistinct blur of white! He tried to cry out, but could only make a harsh, gurgling, hissing sound in the back of his throat. He stared, fascinated, it seemed for hours. Then he heard.

In the same instant the men had seen it. "There he goes!"

In quick succession, so that they were hardly separated, two sharp cracks echoed flatly; and shot rattled against the trunks of trees.

"Got him! We got him!"

"Stone dead, by God!"

They scrambled noisily across the ruins towards the body. They looked down at it silently for a few moments. One of them produced a packet of cigarettes.

"Well, that's the last time this one will take poultry. It's a proper comical-looking beast — white all over, where it isn't dirty. I wonder what breed it is?"

"Mongrel." There was a short laugh. "A trace of greyhound, a trace of everything."

"A trace of the Devil, too. Dogs are worse than foxes when they turn."

They picked up their guns.

Behind the hillock, a small boy lay face downwards. One

leg was doubled under him; the other sprawled out a little to one side. The skin of the knee was torn where it rested on a sharp stone.

Ginny wasn't listening. He was quite still. The taut muscles didn't quiver. The expression on his half-buried, tear-stained face was static. In a little while, his body would begin to grow stiff and cool.

Nineteen Ninety-four

DOCTOR JAMES EDDINGTON SHEAFFER dropped his two-pedal jetomatic bumble-bee to two thousand feet. He allowed it to hover for a few seconds, while he stared disconsolately down at the suburb wondering how his wife, Emily, would receive the Joyful News. Then he murmured listlessly, almost to himself: "Bee, bee, bee! Dive for the hive!"

The micro-transmitter in his wristwatch relayed this routine command to the black box under the bumble-bee's bonnet. The machine hummed dutifully, and began its almost vertical drop to the Sheaffer residence at 793 Hope Boulevard.

Dr. Sheaffer watched his lawn grow from the size of a postage stamp to the dimensions of a bath towel. If only, he thought wistfully, it would come right up and hit him.

This sad yearning for nirvana was a direct result of his recent glorious exit from Independent Electronic Brain Washers Inc. At a conservative estimate, his scalp should have been safe for at least three more years. But, preceded by no more warning than the sudden appearance of an antique marble clock, a box of ten-inch cigars and a magnum of champagne, his dear, loyal colleagues had confronted him with a rigged vote that made him President. The next show of hands accepted the customary resignation which, by some small oversight, he had forgotten to include in his inaugural speech; and the final vote, also unanimous, awarded him a pension of twenty thousand dollars a year, in recognition of distinguished service during his five-minute Presidency.

So now he knew what it felt like to be professionally assassinated. He had often wondered.

These bitter thoughts were terminated by the bumblebee's touchdown at the side of Dr. Sheaffer's heart-shaped roof pool. He climbed out of the bee and hauled a stack of beribboned boxes after him. Three thousand dollars' worth of new dresses for Emily. Dr. Sheaffer's scowl deepened. He had had to stare at a quick-changing robot mannequin — adjusted to Emily's exact size — for almost an hour before they let him sign a cheque.

Meanwhile, the cause of his ordeal by *haute couture* emerged from the house funnel with a happy smile on her lips. She had been down in the kitchen, dialling coffee and doughnuts, when she heard the bee turn into its homing dive. And being eager to display her latest illegal creation — a kind of sari, clumsily fashioned from a lace tablecloth that had belonged to her grandmother and several generations of moths — she had stepped into the funnel, whereupon a copper disc, powered by a column of compressed air, gently blasted her to the roof.

Dr. Sheaffer dropped the boxes and gazed at his wife apprehensively.

"Hi, male," said Emily.

"Hi, female," said Dr. Sheaffer, joining in the ritual greeting.

A glazed nonchalance descended over Emily's face. With practised ease, she whipped through the robot mannequin's basic routine.

"Like it?" she demanded anxiously.

"It's certainly revealing," he conceded. "But for Pete's sake, don't wear it on the roof, Em. Suppose there's a spotter!" He threw a nervous glance at the bee-filled sky.

"Pooh," said Emily. "You don't have to tell *me* to look out for spotters. And, anyway, there's nothing under three thousand feet." She lifted her head and glanced at a steady stream of traffic on the top level. Then, sensing perhaps that something was wrong, she placed her arms round Dr. Sheaffer's neck, snuggled close, bit his ear playfully, and whispered: "What's the matter, darling? Have they cut down your work quota?"

"They have annihilated it," he said, with restrained drama. Emily looked as if someone had just slapped her.

"This morning, my pet," he continued bitterly, "I was elected President, retired with full military honours, and awarded a pension of twenty thousand bucks — all in four minutes flat. And how do you like that?"

Emily didn't like it. Her eyes glistened with tears that were somehow persuaded to defy gravity by sheer will-power.

"But you're only thirty-five, darling. They — they can't do it!"

"They did." There was a certain melancholy satisfaction in Dr. Sheaffer's voice. "Item: One scientist, redundant, sacrificed on the altar of Automation. What say we celebrate tonight and give a decent burial? We'll have the Harrisons over. Joe got his six months ago – but then he was due for it, lucky devil. He was nearly forty-one."

Suddenly, she gripped his arm. "Jimmy, it's illegal! It's just a — horrible mistake. The law says anyone is entitled to work until he's forty."

Dr. Sheaffer smiled a wintry smile. "Article Seven of the Industrial Code. You know what Article Eight says?"

"I didn't even know there was an Article Eight."

"Translated into basic gibberish, my love, it says that if any dim-witted machine can do the job better than a merely intelligent human being, the human is definitely out — regardless of age, sex, colour or creed. Amen."

Emily stared at him unbelievingly for a moment. Then the tears defied gravity no longer. "But — isn't brain-washing classified as a human occupation?" she wailed. "I thought — "

"I thought so, too," he said gently. "But while I was clearing out my locker, they told me about my successor — a positronic robot. He can wash four brains at once. *Independent* paid one million five hundred thousand dollars for him, with a glad heart. At least, it's solved their surplus profits problem for about six months. Then they'll have to buy another robot and fire somebody else." Suddenly, he grinned. "I — er — brought you some new dresses. Interested?"

"Robot rags!" she snapped fiercely. "How I hate them! Why aren't women allowed to make their own clothes, like this lovely sari?"

"Seditious little minx!" He delivered an affectionate pat to her posterior. "You wouldn't be wanting to put half a million rag machines out of work, I hope. Besides, we have to get rid of all our lousy money somehow. Let's have a drink, then I'll call Joe on the plate."

But Emily went to the pile of gown boxes and, after a hurried glance at the sky, kicked them unceremoniously under the tall sunbrella. Secure from inquisitive sky-eyes in the broad circle of shade, she jerked each immaculate dress out of its immaculate wrapping. She gazed at the resulting pile with lips curled, then proceeded to stamp it underfoot, grinding viciously with the tiny heels of her house sabots. Finally, having given the heap of scientifically selected gowns the heel treatment, she knelt down and tried to tear them apart.

Dr. Sheaffer whistled for the dumb waiter, which rolled round the edge of the pool to him like an obedient hound. He dialled himself a highball, sat on the diving-board, and watched Emily with a tolerant smile. The value of her destructive onslaught was chiefly psychological, since all the dresses were created from the synthetic fibre *eternalon* — uncrushable, unstainable, untearable and everlasting. Also guaranteed not to burn.

"Have fun," he said mildly. "You're playing with a mere three thousand bucks' worth."

Panting a little, her wavy blonde hair leaking from its sun-gold fashion sack, Emily threw him a guilty grin.

"If they look a little worn when the Usage Inspector calls, I'll never have to wear them at all," she explained.

Dr. Sheaffer dialled himself another highball, and began to toy with the illusion that he would secretly build his own electronic brain, whose programming he could then wash out whenever the mood took him. There was only one flaw. It would take two years or so to build the brain. He wondered if he would stay interested that long.

Suddenly, a red light flickered on a small screen set in the wall by the roof porch; and the nymphean voice of the auto-announcer said sweetly: "Dr. Sheaffer, you have a visitor. Dr. Sheaffer, you have a visitor."

The screen clouded, then condensed into the image of a tall fat-faced man with a vacant smile that looked as if it had been carved by an air-chisel.

Dr. Sheaffer stared at this apparition and turned slightly pale. Even from his perch by the diving-board, he could see the large circular badge in the stranger's lapel. Its motif was a silver hammer.

"Em, it's the Breaker; and we didn't even get a Warning!"

Emily was in the middle of a quick-change act. She stepped neatly out of her sari, snatched one of the new dresses at random, slipped into it and closed the electro-zip all in one smooth movement. Then she faced her husband guiltily. "Oh, Jimmy, we did get a Warning! Last month. I meant to show it you, but it sort of fell into the disposal chute." She brightened. "But we can send him away again. He's not due till Friday the thirteenth."

Dr. Sheaffer stood up. "Don't tell anyone. Today is Friday the thirteenth."

"Dr. Sheaffer!" snapped the auto-announcer reproachfully.

"Your visitor is waiting."

With the air of a Christian martyr about to fraternise with a lion, he stepped into the funnel and dropped quickly down to the hall. The front door opened automatically as he approached it, and the Breaker stepped forward, jauntily swinging his violin case.

"Dr. Sheaffer? Pleased to meetcha. Well, Doc, it's your turn to get de Hammer again. Time kind of jets like hell, don't it?"

"Does it?" said Dr. Sheaffer bitterly. "This is my favourite nightmare, and it's already too long."

"Haw-haw," roared the Breaker. "Ain't I a social wow?" He opened his violin case and took out the regulation four-pound Hammer. He swung it experimentally, and looked round for the first Obsolete Object. He found it in the combined barometer, calendar and date-box that had hung in the Sheaffer hall for over five years.

"This thing talk?" demanded the Breaker.

"No, but it's an English model," explained Dr. Sheaffer without much hope. "We're rather attached to it."

"Too bad," said the Breaker mournfully. "Regulations say dey gotta talk." He took a mighty swipe with the Hammer. Brass bent, glass tinkled, and a quivering needle swung to 'Very Stormy'. At the same time, the calendar registered January 1st, A.D. 2000, which, as the date-box duly pointed out, was Dr. Sheaffer's maternal great-grandmother's 109th birthday.

"Many happy returns, dear lady," said the Breaker. He switched on a pocket recorder and spoke into his wrist microphone: "Resident: 793 Hope Boulevard. Item: one weather-box. Owner: Sheaffer, James E." Then he switched off, and murmured to Dr. Sheaffer reprovingly: "You gotta keep up wit de times, Doc. Junk is anti-social. Now leave us, as de poet says, seek pastures new."

He prodded Dr. Sheaffer gently with the symbolic

Hammer, so that he backed through the lounge doorway. The Breaker followed with an anticipatory gleam in his eyes.

The first thing he pounced on was the television, a thirty-inch try-di stereophonic model complete with built-in cocktail cabinet and eye-lotion dispenser.

"Pre-hi-storic," announced the Breaker with pity. "Gol-durn it, Doc, you mean to say you been burnin' de little lady's peepers out wit dat?"

"Now, listen," said Dr. Sheaffer angrily, "I happen to like thirty inchers. So does my wife. Besides, this one has functioned perfectly for years. We can get Eurovision on it — London, Paris, Rome — all direct."

"You don't say?" The Breaker was mildly impressed.

A look of glazed disbelief came into Dr. Sheaffer's eyes, as he watched the Hammer hover above the walnut cabinet. With the unhurried air of a connoisseur, the Breaker selected his striking point. The Hammer delivered an almost affectionate tap to the photo-elec remote control dome. It and the cathode tube collapsed in a simultaneous crash. Dr. Sheaffer remained paralysed.

"Amen," murmured the Breaker, and promptly recorded the execution of the Sheaffer television on his pocket tape. Then, with lightning efficiency, he disposed of a 1989 Mity Mijit air-conditioner, and even the out-moded electronic cat-vac that crawled along behind him lapping up all the small debris.

"Hokay," said the Breaker, turning his back on the devastation, "now for de slumber factory, Doc."

By this time, Dr. Sheaffer was vibrating with a soundless, impotent fury. Not only was it definitely illegal to avoid, obstruct, coerce, distract, bribe, mutilate or murder a Breaker; but you could also get six months' social therapy in a psychiatric ward for even arguing with one.

Sadly rejecting a lovely vision of mayhem, Dr. Sheaffer led the way to the funnel.

As they stepped into the bedroom, the Breaker surveyed the double lullabed with professional ecstasy. Its ancient hypno-reel, whose soft music was designed to gently render the patient unconscious, brought a huge grin to his face. Its gas-operated oblivion jets nearly reduced him to hysteria.

"Doc," he said, wiping the tears from his eyes, "yore nights of torture is almost ended. Lullabeds is out. Beambeds is in. Dey have a psychostatic beam dat hits yore pore droopin' brain kerplonk. Knocks you cold in nothin' flat, and also irons out yore worries while you dream."

Dr. Sheaffer closed his eyes as the lullabed received ninety seconds of blitzkrieg. When he opened them, hypno-reel, oblivion jets and slow-rocking coils lay round his feet like squashed metallic flowers.

"Guess dat's all hereabouts," said the Breaker, mercifully reprieving Emily's antique dressing-table. He regarded Dr. Sheaffer benignly. "Doc, you ain't takin' a negative attitude, I hope? I gotta report back if you show a negative attitude."

"Negative attitude? Who — me?" Dr. Sheaffer's sudden display of injured innocence looked more like the onset of a Black Phase in an acute manic-depresssive.

"Sandblast it," said the Breaker, as if reasoning with a precocious four-year-old, "we all gotta be modern, ain't we? I bust de junk, and give you maybe a 10,000 credit. So you hop to de Commissariat and settle for a beambed, a six-foot wall screen, a cat-vac dat plays all de hit tunes of de century, and a weather-squawk dat dispenses seasonal underwear and feeds you chill-pills before you got time to sneeze. Dat's progress. Now ain't it?"

"That sure is progress," murmured Dr. Sheaffer between clenched teeth.

"Well, den" said the Breaker, "leave us continue wit de civilising of dis happy home. Which way to de calorie gallery, Doc?"

Dr. Sheaffer expelled a deep sigh, and took him to the kitchen.

Emily was there, waiting for them. At that moment, she would gladly have exchanged her slim, svelte figure for two hundred pounds of blubber and the silhouette of a bulldozer. She was standing in front of a semi-antique electric washing machine, hoping it wouldn't be noticed.

"How," said the Breaker politely.

"Do," replied Emily, observing the convention with an air of frigidity.

The Breaker pretended not to notice the washing machine. "Say-say-say," he remarked heartily, "dis cook-nook really shines. Selectron-range, infra-toaster and a hi-fi taste restorer. Ain't dat de answer to an ulcer's prayer?"

Yet even as he spoke, he edged a little nearer to the doomed washing machine.

"You missed the corner panel," said Emily, with a note of panic in her voice. "It's the latest deep sleep unit. We got two ducks, five chickens, three lobsters and a turkey all in tenderising coma . . . We're going to let the turkey sleep through till Thanksgiving."

But the gambit failed. Apparently unmoved by the wonder of suspended animation, the Breaker pounced inexorably on his prey. His movement was so sudden that Emily almost cowered.

"Why, Mrs. Sheaffer," he purred, "ain't you de naughty little girl! Riskin' yore reputation for dis old wet-wash box. What would yore psychiatrist say?"

"No!" pleaded Emily in desperation. "Don't hit it, *please*! It's a family heirloom. I know it's obsolete, but . . ." Her voice faded as she watched the Breaker clip the special die-head on the Hammer.

"What shall I book you for, dear lady?" he asked, with a happy smile. "Bribery or obstruction?"

The Hammer rose and crashed down three times. Each

time, the legend OBSOL was stamped on the thin, dented panels. And each time, the Sheaffers winced as if they personally had been dented.

"Lady," said the Breaker, regarding the battered machine, "when de ultrasonic wash box comes, you will remember me wit tears of gratitude."

"You bet!" retorted Dr.Sheaffer grimly. "Tell me, how did a soulless slob like you ever come to be mistakenly classified human? Now book me for sedition, and I'll use the Hammer to burst your obsolete skull!"

Emily went as white as a sheet.

The Breaker let loose a profound sigh. It was his destiny to be universally misjudged.

"If you prick us," he remarked sadly, "do we not bleed? If you tickle us, do we not laugh? If you poison us, do we not die? And if you wrong us, shall we not revenge — Moychant of Venice, Act Tree. Have a heart, Doc. Somebody's gotta do this lousy job." He gave a wicked grin. "Now let's go see yore flivver. A little boyd told me dat it's ready for de big knock."

A triumphant smile spread over Dr. Sheaffer's face. "Prepare yourself for a slight disappointment," he announced. "It's a 1965 Cadillac glassbody — in case you don't know, a scheduled antique."

"You don't say?" The Breaker raised his eyebrows. "Well, likewise prepare yourself for a shock, Doc. De 1965 glass Cad has just been declared obsolete. It ain't roadworthy no more. Sad, ain't it?"

But for Dr Sheaffer it was more than sad; it was the ultimate tragedy. For years he had nursed and cherished the glass Cadillac, spending hundreds of man-hours restoring it from the battered wreck he had discovered in a Minnesota barn to a gleaming showroom specimen. It was the envy of all his friends who, tiring of their 200-miles-an-hour road-bugs, watched the ancient chariot chug along at a sedate ninety with wistful eyes.

The knowledge that it was now due for the Hammer induced a mental trauma which was too heavy for his already overloaded circuits. Somewhere in the cloudy reaches of his brain, a whole row of fuses blew. He spun round twice, dropped in a heap on the kitchen stool, and gaped at the Breaker as if he had just described in detail the approaching end of the world.

The Breaker gazed at him with mild compassion, then turned to Emily and shrugged. "Funny how de men always break foist," he observed clinically. "Maybe it better clobber de Cad while Doc is still dreamin' of home . . . Which way to de death cell, dear lady?"

Emily pointed a trembling finger towards a Dutch door. "First right past the bee-hive," she whispered.

Presently, muffled reverberations told of the Cadillac's swan song. Emily placed her arms protectively round Dr. Sheaffer's hunched shoulders as if to screen him from the unwelcome sound. But strangely, he didn't even flinch.

As the last crash died away, Dr. Sheaffer suddenly pulled himself together. "Em," he said calmly, "maybe we're obsolete, too."

Before she had time to consider the point, the Breaker returned with the air of one who has performed his duty regardless of personal feelings. He entered the kitchen, laid the Hammer nonchalantly against the deep sleep unit, and punched a pocket calculator with clumsy fingers for about forty seconds.

"From the President of the United States, greetings," he announced formally. "On account of de aforementioned executions, Uncle Sam owes you lucky people just twelve thousand five hundred dollars. You got thirty days to spend it." He scooped up the Hammer and returned it to its case. As he turned to go, he patted Dr. Sheaffer on the shoulder. "Now cracks a noble heart. Good-night, sweet prince, and flights of angels sing thee to thy rest — Hamlet Five, Scene Two. Be seein' you Doc!"

The Breaker made his exit with a genial smile.

When he had gone, Dr. Sheaffer kicked a stool over to the kitchen visiplate, sat down and dialled. "Might as well let Joe have the glad tidings," he said dismally.

Then, waiting for the screen to light up, he suddenly grabbed Emily, pulled her on to his knee and closed her startled lips with an unusually passionate kiss. "Just testing reflexes," he explained. "Guess we're still alive." He seemed surprised.

Neither of them noticed when the face appeared on the screen. It regarded them with mute approval for a second or two, then coughed gently. Emily gave a faint squeal, broke away, and faded rapidly into the background.

"Hi, Joe," said Dr. Sheaffer, unperturbed.

"Thanks for the still life," said Joe. "Do I clap or send a donation?"

Dr. Sheaffer made a rude noise. "It's Friday the thirteenth, and I've hit the jackpot. This morning, *Independent* fired me. This afternoon, we had the Breaker."

The smile disappeared from Joe Harrison's face. "You poor people! Jimmy, he didn't hammer the — "

"He sure did. One glass Cad, obsolete. Also Em's washing machine and a few other vintage pieces."

"Hell," said Joe inadequately. "My heart bleeds for you. Why don't you have dinner with us this evening? We'll cry into each other's hemlock."

"We were going to invite you and Patty thisaways."

"Inappropriate," said Joe. "After a couple of beers, we'd be giving artificial respiration to the Cadillac's corpse—slightly illegal. Also, I have something I want to show you, I think. How about it?"

"Love to," said Dr. Sheaffer. "What time shall we dive?"

"Shall we say eight?"

"You just said it. Over and out."

"I leave you with this thought: Time is a wonderful healer.

Over and out." Joe Harrison gave an enigmatic grin and switched off. The screen went blank.

The sky was shot through with hard, bright stars; but they were no match for the electric constellations of suburbia, spreading out a thousand feet below the bumble-bee in all directions. Gazing through the canopy, Emily tried in vain to pick out the Harrison residence from that bewildering multi-coloured glare.

She had already recovered somewhat from the destruction of her cherished washing machine. As a gesture of defiance, she was wearing her home-made sari once more, discreetly camouflaged by a white foam-fur coat.

Dr. Sheaffer dialled the Harrisons' landing beam. He was pleasantly surprised when the 'beam engaged' signal told him that he was practically riding down it already. Allowing the black box to take over for touchdown, he turned to his wife and said: "To hell with it all, Em. We still have us."

She found his hand in the darkness, and squeezed it gently.

Thirty seconds later, Joe and Patty, who were waiting on the roof, met them with a volley of greetings and vague sympathetic noises.

They all crowded into the funnel and dropped down to the dining-room, where Patty gazed with unfeigned admiration at Emily's sari.

"My dear, it's absolutely four-dimensional! Wherever did you get the pattern?"

"I sort of dreamed it up," said Emily modestly.

Joe inspected it with scientific detachment. "It reminds me of the Nitz-Suvarov concept of sub-space," he remarked profoundly.

"What's that?" asked Emily.

"A series of holes tied together with theories. Have a shot of this Breaker's Blood, Jimmy. Six jiggers equal total amnesia."

"To the destruction of Utopia," growled Dr. Sheaffer, downing his cocktail with a single swallow. There was a long pause. "What's the formula, Joe?" he enquired reverently. "Rocket fuel and ether?"

"Right first time. Hot jets, brother!" Joe emptied his own glass, blinked twice and counted slowly. By the time he reached nine, the red mists had drifted away.

Patty regarded the men severely. "All right, break up the suicide session, Dinner is just about at firing point."

Half an hour later, when they had disposed of quantities of seafood cunningly disguised as tropical fruit, followed by a dessert of vitamin-laden Angel Bubbles, Dr. Sheaffer took advantage of a lull in the conversation to bring up the subject that lay most heavily on his mind.

"Joe, what in Hades am I going to do with it all?"

"With all what, Brother Misfit?"

"All the damned leisure provided by this lousy Golden Age."

Joe threw an odd half-smile at Patty, and stalled. "Them's hard words, Mister. Almost treasonable, in fact."

Dr. Sheaffer moodily helped himself to another shot of Breaker's Blood. "Three cheers for treason," he remarked calmly, "plus a few Hosannas for sabotage. That's what this world needs — a spot of good, clean sabotage. Nothing violent, Joe. Just the simple liquidation of two or three thousand robot factories. Then you and I and all the other hasbeens could start work again."

Patty suddenly stood up. She exchanged glances with Joe. Dr. Sheaffer got the impression that they had reached a silent and obscure agreement.

"Come along, Em," she said. "Let's leave these two rebels to their sedition. I never told you about my secret wardrobe, did I? Come and see what I have been doing for the last six months."

She took a somewhat puzzled Emily by the arm and led her out of the room.

Dr. Sheaffer subjected Joe to a long and searching gaze.

"Seems to me somebody is being downright dishonest — I hope. And not only about dressmaking, either. I wish you'd tell me what it's all about, Joe — unless," he added bitterly, "you don't trust me."

Joe Harrison poured himself a double transfusion of Breaker's Blood. "Hell, this thing is so big, I don't even trust myself. But before I pull you in at the deep end, let's see if we really are two minds with a single warp."

"Fair enough. Jet!"

"Proposition one: we think ninety-five per cent automation is carrying the virtue of laziness just a shade too far."

"Agreed."

"Proposition two: we want freedom to work as well as freedom to play."

"Agreed."

"Proposition three: we want to earn our living *and* our self-respect, and we don't want charity — not even twenty-thousand-dollars-a-year charity."

"Agreed."

"Proposition four: we question the right of any Federal Department to declare any of our goods and chattels obsolete. We also question the right of said Department to exist."

"Encore."

"Proposition five: we would like to bust the system painlessly, and start all over again — except that we haven't yet worked out a good formula."

"Agreed."

"Proposition six: we are lousy, anti-social rebels — and too maladjusted to enjoy the benefits of this wonderful, wonderful world."

"Carried unanimously."

Joe took a swig of the Breaker's Blood and hiccupped. "Good. James Eddington Sheaffer, I hereby elect you a genuine *bona fide* refugee. And I therefore sentence you to a hundred years transportation — retrospective."

"Carried unanimously," agreed Dr. Sheaffer. "What in hell do you mean?"

Joe grinned and kicked his chair back. "Psst! Follow me, refugee. I have been working on an escape route." He led the way into the hall. There, they stepped into the funnel and dropped down to the games room.

In his enforced leisure, Professor Joseph Harrison, later Director of the Department of Sub-atomic Physics at American Solar Engines Inc., had concentrated his genius on transforming the games room into a replica of a late nineteenth-century bar. He had also added one or two interesting refinements.

"Spittoon, sawdust, genuine gaslight," he said proudly. "Only the liquor is *ersatz.* How do you like it?"

"Wonderful!" Dr. Sheaffer sighed. "Those were the days. But about the escape route — I'm still a trifle fogged."

Joe stepped up to the bar. "Excuse my dramatic sense," he said. Then, facing a wall-length mirror behind the bar, he called "Open Sesame!" The whole wall slid away, revealing a small physics laboratory packed with apparatus.

Dr. Sheaffer stared, open-mouthed.

"Rigged it with an electronic sound-key," explained Joe calmly, "just to baffle any uninvited parties. Here, take a look at this." He displayed a fat metal cylinder about three feet high.

"Looks like an ultrasonic washer," said Dr. Sheaffer, inspecting a couple of small dials with curious calibrations.

"That, dear lawbreaker, is the drive unit of the first chronocar." Joe eased it to one side. "Now, take a look at this."

He pointed to a large plexiglass dome. Its transparent walls, with the exception of a small circular door near the base, were latticed with an intricate system of green, blue and yellow wiring.

"This," continued Joe, after a reverent pause, "is the chronocar itself."

Dr. Sheaffer gazed at it. "Seems more like a cage for a king-size parrot with homicidal tendencies," he announced after careful consideration. "But, if you say it's a chronocar, I'll agree it's a damn fine chronocar. Now what in Hades *is* a chronocar?"

Joe withered him with a glance. "In plain language, my illiterate friend, a time machine."

"A *what*?"

"You heard me. And now, let's join the ladies. The way I tell it, it's a long story." He took a dazed Dr. Sheaffer by the arm and gently propelled him out of the lab. Then Joe casually murmured: "Abracadabra." The whole wall slid smoothly back into position.

Dr. Sheaffer blinked, and stared at the undisturbed nineteenth-century bar. "That Breaker's Blood is really something," he said in an awed voice.

Meanwhile, Emily was inspecting Patty's illegal wardrobe. It consisted of two tight-fitting ankle-length dresses — one in brilliant emerald green and the other in royal blue. Also two enormous hats, one of which looked like a small ostrich farm and the other like a piled-up fruit bowl.

Emily was entranced by these superb creations that would have been the height of fashion around 1900. But her amazement hit boiling point when Patty, blushing with pride, displayed further treasures — to wit: a couple of men's grey suits with stovepipe trousers; a pair of real linen shirts with two-inch starched collars; two dashing crimson cravats; and a brace of straw boaters.

In response to the avalanche of questions, Patty said, mysteriously: "Joe and I are planning a sort of holiday — a permanent one. We're hoping you and Jimmy might be interested. I ought to warn you, though, it's definitely a one-way trip."

"Patty, you're killing me by inches! Tell all before I bust!"

Patty grinned mischievously: "Lady, it's a real tall one, and I wouldn't want to spoil Joe's party piece. I expect he is already breaking it gently to Jimmy. Let's go see."

In the lounge, Professor Joseph Harrison revealed the basic facts about his chronocar and its treasonable purpose. Being the first time machine, he explained, it had the usual limitations of an experimental job. It could transport backwards only; its extreme range being about a hundred years. But the great thing was that it presented a means of escape from the world of 1994; from the frustrating Age of Plenty, the boring Era of Prosperity — from the world fit for robots to live in.

"So we can go back to the pre-atomic age," concluded Joe cheerfully, "before automation and solar power were substituted for sheer guts. Think what it means, Jimmy! If we want to, you and I can half-kill ourselves working twelve hours a day, six days a week, fifty weeks a year. We can work till we're ninety. No human scrap-heap for us!"

"We can make our own clothes," added Patty joyfully. "Trunkloads of 'em. We can cook our own food, darn socks, make curtains, buy old furniture, and have nice smoky fires in the winter. We can read O. Henry by lamplight, and wear the most fantastic undies."

"No Breakers," murmured Emily with a glazed look in her eyes. "No robot-rags. Oh, doesn't it sound wonderful!"

But Dr. Sheaffer was meditating upon larger issues. "Joe," he said dreamily, "how would you like to take a trip out to Kitty Hawk and give the Wright Brothers the lowdown on aerodynamics? Or maybe slip over to Detroit and iron out production problems on the Model T Ford? Or jet — I mean sail — across to England and drop a few hints to Marconi? Later on, of course, we might even drift into movies. You're sure this — this chronocar will do its stuff, Joe? I don't think I'd survive the disappointment."

"Eliminate the anxiety," retorted Joe with confidence. "I've shaken all the bugs out of it. You don't think I would flog an inferior product, do you?"

"No, but — "

"I have calibrations so accurate," pursued Joe, "that we could set course for New Year's Day, 1900, and get there while the champagne corks were still poppin'."

Emily was almost dancing with excitement. "Why don't we?" she asked breathlessly. "Why don't we do just that?"

Joe gave Dr. Sheaffer a searching look. "What do you say, Jimmy? If you want proof that the chronocar can do its stuff, we'll have to stick around while you brush up your mathematics to deal with such sweet topics as the concept of infinite duration in a transfinite space-frame series. Or are you willing to trust me, pal?"

"Hell, no!" said Dr. Sheaffer with a grin. "But I'll take a risk."

"Then what are we waiting for?" said Patty, calmly pouring four shots of Breaker's Blood. "There's no time like the present."

"Dead right," said Emily gaily. "Which is why we're heading for the past."

They raised their glasses in a solemn toast.

"Now," said Joe, suddenly businesslike, "gather round, children, and let's get organised. Patty, you have a list of all the things we need. You and Em go hunt 'em out, while Jimmy and I dismantle the chronocar. Then it's going to take all four of us to load it into the bees. If we use both of 'em, we can do it in one trip."

"Do what in one trip?" asked Dr. Sheaffer.

"Get the chronocar into the desert, genius. You wouldn't want us to emerge on New Year's Day, 1900, in somebody's parlour, now, would you? It could be embarrassing, if not downright awkward."

Presently, the Harrison residence became a hive of activity.

It was long after midnight when the two bumble-bees soared away into a darkness dominated, now, chiefly by stars. As they watched the dimmed faces of cities and suburbs glide mutely below them, the four self-elected refugees felt neither regret nor guilt, but only a delicious sense of freedom, like children playing truant.

They landed in the desert a couple of hours before dawn. They landed near a sad and shadowy ghost town that would come back to life once more only when the calendar had been rolled right back.

"Well, this is it," said Joe happily. "The point of no return."

"Also the reverse," observed Dr. Sheaffer laconically.

While the men reassembled the chronocar and drive unit by the bees' groundlights, Emily and Patty changed into period costume and tried on those wonderful top-heavy bonnets.

The dresses were tight and unyielding in various interesting places. They allowed for no bending, no stretching and precious little breathing. But they felt like the plumage of paradise. Ten minutes before sunrise, the chronocar was assembled and ready for the big vanishing trick. Patty brought out coffee and sandwiches — a last symbolic meal in 1994.

"Dawn's pretty near, now," remarked Joe, bolting a last mouthful of chicken. "We'd better get lost in time, before the buzzing starts. Too bad if a G-bee comes along. I'd hate to meet a spotter crew right now."

Dr. Sheaffer looked at his wife and grinned. He thought she was definitely appealing in the bright green taffeta sheath, and with a fruit bowl on her head. "No regrets, Em? It's still not too late."

Emily smiled, and threw the empty picnic hamper towards

the silent bumble-bee. "No regrets," she said. "Utopia is where you find it."

For A.D. 1994, it was a fitting epitaph; for the imminent world of 1900, it was an optimistic greeting.

Joe and Patty had already entered the chronocar. Dr. Sheaffer kissed his wife very gently and took her by the hand. Presently, they too were safely aboard — locked in a tiny caravel, captained by Professor Joseph Harrison, the new Columbus of Time.

The red rim of the sun showed over the horizon. Joe looked at the instruments on the drive unit, and began to count off seconds very quietly. Then he threw the switch. For a moment, the desert seemed to shimmer in a clear dawn light; then suddenly, there was an endless, flickering succession of days and nights, a backward tornado of change. Even with eyes closed and hands over ears, the four time-jumpers could not shut out the monotonous flashings of the sun, the dancing pattern of stars, or the roaring of an almighty wind.

But at last, the time-jump reached its end, and the desert and the sky were still once more. Joe opened his eyes and stared blankly at the panel of instruments. "Well, I'll be hammered!" he exclaimed in sheer amazement. "The darn thing really worked!"

Presently, four startled people stepped out of the chronocar into a world that was poised on the edge of a new day, a new year and a new century.

Dr. Sheaffer looked towards what had been in the world of 1994 a silent ghost town. But it was a ghost town no longer. It had emerged from the backward resurrection in a riot of noise and light, symbolic of the turbulent and optimistic world of 1900.

"Look!" said Dr. Sheaffer, his voice filled with enthusiasm and awe. "History is already upon us!"

Hand in hand, the four refugees — fugitives from a Utopia

that had failed—prepared to enter an age that, for all its limitations, was an age of opportunity . . .

A strange and busy world. An untidy and reckless world. Too untidy, yet, to be subdued by the orderly zeal of the Planners; too reckless to be tranquillised by the concept of Absolute Security; too busy to reject the dreams and energies of men.

M 81: Ursa Major

Motion does not tire anybody. With the earth as our vehicle we are travelling at twenty miles a second round the sun; the sun carries us at twelve miles a second through the galactic system; the galactic system bears us at 250 miles a second amid the spiral nebulae; . . . If motion could tire, we ought to be dead tired.

Sir Arthur Eddington
The Nature of the Physical World

IT WAS TWENTY hours, ship's time, after firing point. A million miles astern, the earth shone coldly like a small green moon. On the navigation deck of the *Santa-Maria*, a profound silence was disturbed only by the steady but discreet ping of the radio probe.

Captain Mauris leaned back on his contour-berth and waited patiently for his soul to catch up with his body. His sensations at the beginning of each deep voyage were invariably the same. His body had learned to adapt to a force of 10 G and to a stellar acceleration whose graph was a mad ascending curve; but his spirit, while hardly weak, retained the old subconscious reluctance. It didn't much care for the big jump. It would hang tenaciously on to the illusion that Captain Mauris would presently wake up to find himself at home in bed.

He rarely did; because, more often than not, the dream

became the reality. Recently he had calculated that he had slept on earth not more than nine thousand times in his life, whereas he had voyaged among the stars for nearly twice that number of earth-nights. It was the sort of calculation that he did not care to remember — which was principally why he could not forget it.

Which was the dream — earth or space? After twenty hours of space-flight in planetary drive (which nowadays the younger men humorously called first gear) Captain Mauris was not too sure of the answer. He had long ago ceased to have physical space-sickness; but he had never lost the spiritual variety. And lately it had seemed to intensify. Perhaps he was just getting old. Perhaps he really would make this the last trip . . .

The captain sighed, and took refuge in the monumental assumption of Descartes: *I think, therefore I exist*. He began to wonder if the same could be said of his boat-load of physicists. With a sardonic smile, Captain Mauris decided that he had seen terrestrial positronic robots which could lay a greater claim to individuality.

Ever since the dim distant days of the twentieth century, when the scientific caste system had been formalised, physicists had tended to become less and less human; and now they were hardly more than semi-substantial extrapolations of their own theories.

They were a race apart. Watching them board the *Santa-Maria*, listening to their conversation, Captain Mauris had actually wondered whether they might be the new type of omega robots which, according to rumour, were now past the experimental stage. But he had seen two of them playing chess so badly, and a third so delightfully green with space-sickness, that he had regretfully concluded that they were human. Even *sigma* robots played chess excellently; and clearly there was no reason why the robot engineers should endow their offspring with uncontrollable nervous systems.

The physicists, then, were unfortunately human — a sad comment on the sort of civilisation that allowed robots to take charge of global production, while turning the best human brains into second-rate electronic calculators.

The captain's private soliloquy was interrupted by Phylo, the first officer, climbing down from the astrodome.

"Dead on," said Phylo. "Heading straight for *Zeta* of the Great Bear. When do we change gear, Captain?"

Captain Mauris gave him a sour look. "While I command the *Santa-Maria*, Mr. Phylo, we will not change gear."

"Sorry, sir. When do we use the stellar drive, then?"

"I think," replied the captain, "that I will shortly enquire if the physicists are still alive; and if so, when they will be prepared to take the bump."

Phylo laughed. "I hope you're disappointed, sir."

"Meaning what?"

"I hope they're still kicking. I should hate to have to return to earth and explain why we knocked off six top S.F.P.s."

"The world," said Captain Mauris soberly, "might even smell somewhat sweeter for the loss of a few spaceframe physicists. Man is becoming just a little too clever."

"I wonder why you volunteered for the trip, then," said Phylo slyly. "A voyage with S.F.P. men for unspecified experimental purposes hardly promises to be uneventful. Besides, there's the triple danger money — just like the old days when they first tried out the stellar drive."

"Of the few parts of the world that remain unspoiled by civilisation, the Amazonian hinterland is the most attractive — for me," said Captain Mauris obliquely. "One of these days, Phylo, I shall buy myself ten thousand acres in the middle of nowhere. And then, the only time I shall ever take my feet off terra firma will be when I climb into my hammock. The reason I signed on as Master of the *Santa-Maria* is quite simple. It represents almost five thousand acres."

"If," said Philo drily, "we survive whatever tricks the S.F.P.s. are cooking up."

"Exactly," said Captain Mauris. "But it is my firm intention to survive."

Phylo gazed through the plastiglass anti-glare dome at a swarm of hard, unwinking suns. Finally, without looking at Mauris, he said softly: "I think there's also another reason, sir."

"Do you, now!" The captain's tone was not encouraging.

Phylo took a deep breath and ploughed on. "They told me back at base that you were the first skipper to use the stellar drive successfully."

"A slight exaggeration," said Mauris with a cold smile. "I was merely the first captain to return and collect his pay envelope. However, proceed."

"I notice," said Phylo uneasily, "that there's a parallel set of gears — I mean dual controls — on the main panel."

"Well?"

"I don't understand the calibrations on the dials under the lightometer. Nor do I understand why the second bank of meters should have all their throw-in switches locked and sealed."

"An interesting little mystery," observed the captain non-committally. "As you have obviously given some thought to it, what conclusion do you draw?"

"Well, sir," said Phylo hesitantly, "bearing in mind that the *Santa-Maria* has a cargo of S.F.P.s, a skipper who successfully tested the stellar drive, a set of new instruments, and the fact that we are under sealed orders, I think there's only one possible conclusion."

"I should be interested to hear it," said Captain Mauris.

"There have been rumours," continued Phylo, "of a galactic drive. My guess is that the *Santa-Maria* has been fitted out for a trial run. What do you think, sir?"

"I think," replied Captain Mauris, glancing at the bulkhead electrochron, "that I shall shortly break the seal and discover what the Fates have in store for us. I'll tell you this, though — I don't think we shall be experimenting with a galactic drive."

"Why not, sir?"

"Because," said Captain Mauris with a thin smile, "the United Space Corporation has already developed it — as a logical extension of the stellar drive."

Phylo gazed at him in sheer amazement. "It's the first I've heard of it, sir."

"I know," said Mauris imperturbably. "It's still on the secret list. But as I travelled as a paid observer on the test jump, I can definitely assure you that the galactic drive is a fact."

Phylo's voice was filled with awe. "Would it be indiscreet to enquire what distance you logged?"

"Not now," said the captain. "I think — in view of our position — that it will do no harm to give you the facts. We—er—had a little jaunt round *Beta Centauri.*"

"Godalmighty!"

"A matter of seven hundred light-years for the round trip,"added Mauris complacently.

"How long did it take?" demanded Phylo incredulously.

The captain permitted a note of pride to enter his voice. "Three hours, twenty-seven minutes, ship's time — starting and finishing in the neighbourhood of Pluto's orbit."

"Were there any — any casualties?"

"All of us," said Captain Mauris soberly. "We couldn't stop laughing for two days. But I forgot. There was one serious casualty: Egom, the navigator. His star maps were damn near useless, of course. He swore we'd never get home. And when we finally hit the system, the relief was too much for him. He was the only one who didn't stop laughing. And from what I hear, he's still enjoying himself."

Phylo couldn't make up his mind whether or not Captain

Mauris was having a private joke. After a moment or two, he said in a matter-of-fact voice: "I wonder what the hell is going to happen on this trip, then?"

"Probably," said Captain Mauris, "we shall cease to exist."

Four hours later, in the privacy of his cabin, the captain of the *Santa-Maria* broke the seal on a slim envelope and read his instructions. He skipped impatiently through the conventional wording until he came to the part that mattered. He went through it carefully, word for word, three times. The final paragraph gave him a certain grim amusement.

While the normal articles of space-travel obtain for this experimental voyage, there must of necessity be a fluid definition of the Safety Clause. Clearly the primary responsibility of the Master for the safety of his ship and all personnel must be to some extent subordinated by the actual programme sanctioned by the Field Testing Executive of the United Space Corporation. It is not implied, however, that the prerogative of Master's Discretion will inevitably be superseded by test requirements. If the Master should satisfy himself, and the authorised scientists concerned, that the danger factor is sufficient to render the ship's safe return as improbable, therefore neutralising the validity of the experiment, he is entitled to cancel the test programme and return immediately to base. A Court of Enquiry will evaluate the circumstances leading to such a decision. It is, however, earnestly hoped that scientific and ship personnel will so co-operate as to bring both the experiment and the voyage to a successful conclusion.

"Why the devil," said Captain Mauris to himself, "do they use a lot of big words to tell me that I'm merely acting wet-nurse for a bunch of S.F.P.s? *If the Master should satisfy himself, and the authorised scientists concerned*. Very funny!

The whole idea is not less than one hundred per cent suicidal; and then they talk about a sufficient danger factor!"

There was a knock at the door.

"Come in," called Mauris.

It was Kobler, chief of the S.F.P. team. He was a thin pasty-faced man of perhaps forty. His mouth looked as if it would split if he tried to smile.

Mauris motioned him into a chair, and reached for two glasses and the decanter. As he poured the drinks, Kobler glanced at the ship's articles lying on the desk.

"I see you have been studying the scriptures," said the physicist.

"I was merely trying to find out," explained Captain Mauris equably, "what authority, if any, I possess — in case of an emergency."

"And have you found out?" enquired Kobler, sipping his whisky.

"Yes."

"Are you satisfied?"

"No. From the point of view of getting a clear-cut definition, it's as woolly as hell."

"I shouldn't worry, if I were you," said Kobler pleasantly. "If anything goes wrong, you'll probably have a megasecond in which to think a last beautiful thought."

"That," retorted Mauris thinly, "is why I would have liked sufficient power to overrule you people — just in case I happened to anticipate the hypothetically fatal megasecond."

"Sorry," said Kobler, "but I'm the boss-man. That's the way it has to be for this sort of thing. You'd better resign yourself to praying for my spiritual guidance."

"I don't know why you people need a space-captain," said Mauris testily. "You could have programmed the *Santa-Maria* to take you to dissolution point under her own steam."

Kobler smiled, and his face didn't crack. "You may not believe it," he said ironically, "but we space-frame gentry have nice orderly minds. We're very conventional really. Besides, even a space-captain has his uses. How did you enjoy the hop round *Beta Centauri*?"

"So that was why they wanted me to go," said Mauris. "I wondered about it."

"You were lucky," said Kobler. "They wouldn't let me go because some idiot mathematician suggested that the ship might surface too near a sun, or something damn silly like that. It seems that my brain was considered too valuable to be fried."

"Mine evidently wasn't," observed the captain.

"You, my friend, are unique," said Kobler drily. "You are a veteran of the stellar drive and the galactic jump. We regard you as a curio, a kind of talisman."

"I am flattered," said Captain Mauris. "And now, I think, we had better discuss ways and means."

"You know the destination?" asked Kobler.

The captain inclined his head towards the papers on the desk. "According to the *Field Testing Executive*," he said calmly, "it is *Messier 81*."

"What do you think of it?" asked Kobler smugly.

"I think it might be — interesting," said Captain Mauris with sarcasm. "I don't think I've ever visited a spiral nebula before."

Kobler grinned. "One million six hundred thousand light-years," he said. "Quite a little hop when you come to think of it."

"How long do you think it will take?"

The physicist's grin broadened. "I don't know," he said happily. "Probably just that hypothetically fatal megasecond."

Mauris restrained himself with an effort. "I'd appreciate a brief exposition of the theory," he said. "It might be useful."

Kobler helped himself to more whisky, leaned back in his chair and regarded the ceiling. "Essentially," he began, "it involves my private theory of matter, which also involves the stress characteristic of space and the so-called temporal regression."

"Proceed," said Mauris. "For a moment, I thought you were going to get complicated."

Kobler ignored him. "You understand, of course," he continued, "that matter is a form of locked-up energy?"

"Yes."

"Good. I now have news for you. Energy is simply a form of locked-up space. There is, from the physicist's point of view, quite a reasonable amount of energy in the cosmos: there is also the devil of a lot of space. Now there is, as well, the curious phenomenon of the expansion and unwrinkling of space alongside the actual diminution of energy."

"You wouldn't be throwing overboard the first and second laws of thermodynamics, would you?" interrupted the captain mildly.

Kobler admired his own finger-nails complacently.

"Child's play," he said. "Entropy and the first and second laws are all washed up. Funny thing, when I was a student I instinctively knew there was something wrong. But back to the point. I have established a definite coefficient — the practical application of which means, my friend, that we too can adopt the charming habit of energy. We can *submerge* in space. Just as energy, when it thinks nobody is looking, opens a little door into the fifth dimension and smartly side-steps all detection by *becoming* space, so we can play the same trick. Only we can go one better: we can become energy again. Which, in effect, means that we can knock the mainspring out of time. Because, Captain Mauris, by becoming virtually non-existent, we escape the temporal regression. That, in a simpler fashion, is why you were able to hop round *Beta Centauri* and swallow seven hundred light-years. And of the three hours twenty-seven minutes it took, you spent most of the time surfacing so that Egon could panic over his star maps."

"That is true," said Mauris. "But — if you will forgive a simple space-captain for pointing out the obvious — we were functioning in a known energy system. By making the new target M 81, you are postulating a jump clean out of the local energy pattern."

"Not *out* of, but *through*," corrected the physicist. "On the *Beta Centauri* trip you were still slightly limited by a temporal regression. This time, the deceleration will be so sharp as to make a total breakthrough. We shall make a neat hole in our own space frame and enter sub-space. We shall become a pattern of space on the frame of sub-space. Then we shall localise our return breakthrough when a pretty little instrument that I have programmed for M 81 recognises the surface energy patterm."

"Suppose the programming fails."

Kobler laughed. "As it is the first true cosmometer, there is the possibility. But you can take it from me that it is theoretically perfect."

Captain Mauris thought nostalgically of the Amazonian hinterland. After nearly a minute's silence, he said: "It's nice to feel that somebody's confident, anyway."

"Space has a very definite direction," pursued Kobler. "Its vortices are the galactic leaks. In some respects, we can regard the sub-echoes of nebulae as stepping-stones. In the extra-galactic jump, it's chiefly a question of defining the direction/deceleration crisis — or, in plain language, of making the right hole at the right time."

"I expect you'll want to clear the System before the — er — experiment begins," ventured Mauris.

"Naturally," said Kobler. "By the way, would you like me to tell the crew what it's all about?"

"I was going to suggest a brief lecture," replied Mauris. "But since you have explained the background to me so lucidly, I think I might save you that little job. I'll tell them we're going to make a nice little hole in the balloon of space and pop up again sixteen hundred thousand light-years away. That should make for some interesting discussion."

"You think they'll panic?"

The captain shook his head. "They'll just laugh politely, and think I'm getting too old for the job."

"So far as I can see," said Kobler, downing the remainder of his whisky, "everything is predictable — except the human reaction."

"It makes for a nice philosophical problem," observed Mauris.

"What does?"

"Whether or not we can be conscious of our own non-existence."

Kobler gave him a look of respect. "That's the crux of the matter," he admitted. "You see, the *Santa-Maria* and all aboard will cease to be a system of molecular organisations."

"Conversely," said the captain in a matter-of-fact voice, "it will become the abstract memory of an energy pattern which will be re-synthesised out of space — when and if your infallible cosmometer correlates the pattern of M 81 with that of its own environment."

Kobler sat up. "I didn't know you were a physicist."

"I'm not," retorted Mauris drily. "But I'll tell you something else, too. It's going to be damn cold!"

Pluto's orbit was a hundred million miles astern, and the *Santa-Maria* had achieved a satisfactory clearance of the System. For the last ten hours, she had voyaged under her stellar drive. Through the dark plastiglass port-holes, men occasionally stared at the long star-torn silence of total night.

The navigation deck was a scene of activity and tension, for deceleration point was rapidly approaching. A fat copper cylinder had been battened to the deck in front of the main control panel; and the second bank of switches, with their mysterious calibrations, had now been unsealed. Kobler had lovingly supervised the installation of his cosmometer, and was now displaying sufficient humanity to fuss about it much as an anxious father nursing his first-born. Phylo, the first officer, was surreptitiously biting his nails. He was definitely unhappy. His appreciation of the science of physics being rather more limited than usual for one in his position, he had come to believe simply that the approaching experiment was merely the most elaborate method yet invented of committing suicide.

Of all the personnel of the *Santa-Maria*, Captain Mauris was the most calm. He was very busy breaking several regulations. He lay on his Master's contour-berth and watched all the extra berths that were needed by the physicists being bolted down. Kobler had decided, after much consultation, that the entire S.F.P. team should foregather on the navigation deck for the experiment. Half a dozen extra berths had then been hastily erected, giving the impression of a surrealist hospital.

Normally, Captain Mauris would have regarded the invasion with frigid resentment. But now he watched the proceedings with a benevolent air.

It was his duty as Master of the ship to present at all times an aspect of confidence. With the aid of a bottle of Scotch and a somewhat prehistoric corncob pipe, he was fulfilling this obligation admirably. He was also sweating, for he had discarded his uniform jacket in favour of two old polo-necked jerseys. Doubtless the *Field Testing Executive* would strongly disapprove of his unconventional approach, but then the F.T.E. were millions of miles away.

Having taken what he considered to be a sufficiency of spirit, the captain was now engaged in chewing glucose tablets. Phylo watched him with silent awe.

Eventually, Kobler looked up from his cosmometer. "Nine minutes to go, Captain," he said formally.

Mauris glanced at the bulkhead electrochron and nodded. "Five hundred seconds," he said pleasantly. "And then sixteen hundred thousand light-years. Science is quite wonderful."

Kobler was nettled. "What are you eating — nerve pills?"

"Glucose," said Mauris affably. "I've been dieting on whisky and glucose."

"Why?"

"Because," explained Mauris, "I intend to keep both warm and energetic."

"There should not be any drop in temperature," said Kobler. "In any case, the thermostat will fix it."

"The non-existent thermostat," corrected Mauris gently. "But I was not thinking of coldness that can be measured in degrees centigrade."

"There is no other," said Kobler authoritatively. "Neither is there any need to keep your strength up. There will be no fatigue."

"Nor was I thinking of physical fatigue."

Kobler shrugged. "Every man to his own superstitions," he said.

Captain Mauris smiled. "Would it be indiscreet to suggest that yours are non-Euclidean?"

Kobler turned away in disgust and spoke to one of his aides. "Get everyone in their contour-berths and switch the auto-announcer on. We might as well let the brain take over."

Captain Mauris made a last attempt to be helpful.

"It is well known," he said placidly, "that smooth motion never made anybody tired. But I am not so sure about smooth stillness. It may be very fatiguing. Perhaps it may even be possible for a non-existent man to be too tired to maintain his non-existent bodily heat. Would you care for some glucose?"

Kobler did not turn round, but his shoulders shook

convulsively. Captain Mauris interpreted the movement as one of silent laughter.

"One minute to deceleration-point," boomed the auto-announcer.

Men with strained faces lay strapped on their contour berths awaiting the indefinable shock of total stillness. They stared with unseeing eyes at their neighbours; at the bulk-head; at the fat ominous copper cylinder. Phylo's lips were quivering; Captain Mauris, in spite of his light-hearted precautions, felt a strange icy finger probing his heart; even Kobler's massive confidence wavered as the critical moment drew near.

"Forty-five seconds," said that damnably calm automatic voice. "Thirty seconds . . . fifteen seconds . . . ten, nine, eight, seven, six, five, four, three, two, one — zero!"

And then there was nothing – no lurch, no pressure, no sudden stress. Only a great vacancy; a sensation of utter darkness; a sharp instantaneous dream of unbeing; and then only the bare memory of the dream.

In the dimensions of physical space, the *Santa Maria* and all aboard her had ceased to exist. Where, before, a tiny metallic capsule — a caravel of explorers — had surged out from the dust-like brood of planets circling one of the innumerable suns, there was now nothing. The track of a strange silver bullet, coursing at a fantastic speed that was yet a mere snail's pace through the long deserts of the home galaxy, had stopped suddenly. There was no wreckage: there were no survivors. For what had existed in the apparent reality of space-time was now as if it had never been . . .

Captain Mauris was alone. He was alone because there was nothing else. He was alone with the illusion of his own existence. The stillness had settled like a slow inward frost.

His premonition was justified. In a vacancy of non-sensation, there was yet the overwhelming weight of a curious fatigue — as if, at the moment of deceleration, the material cosmos had suddenly become too tired to hold together. As if Mauris himself must support the tiredness of a phantom universe.

"So this is what it's like to be dead," he mumbled in a sleepy voice. He was surprised. He was pulled up with a sickening jolt. He had heard his own voice, reverberating as in an empty room. The voice that followed was less of a shock than this disturbing mockery of survival.

"Captain Mauris! Captain Mauris! Soon you will be too tired to be dead, too cold to be an illusion. For you are condemned to be reborn."

It was a woman's voice, low, musical; drifting without urgency through the deep canyons of unbeing.

Mauris listened, appalled. It was a voice he recognised — the voice of a woman he might have married: a familiar voice, belonging to one he had never known.

"Who are you?" he called desperately, hearing the words echo on a wall of blackness.

There was laughter tumbling through the emptiness of stars. "Mary Smith," said the voice, "Betty Jones and Pearl White. Marie-Antoinette, Cleopatra, Helen of Troy."

"I am mad!" cried Captain Mauris. "The stars are dark, and still there is something left to dream."

"You are unborn," said the voice gently. "Have patience."

Captain Mauris tried to move and could not; for there was nothing to move, no location to be changed.

"Who am I?" he shouted wildly.

"Captain Mauris."

"There is no Captain Mauris," he yelled savagely. "He is unborn, therefore he has never lived!"

"You are learning," came the answer, softly. "You are learning that it is necessary to wait."

"Who am I?" he demanded urgently.

The laughter came like an invisible tide, sweeping him on

its crest. "Punchinello," said the voice gaily, "Prometheus, Simple Simon, Alexander the Great."

"Who am I?" he called insistently.

"You are no one. Who knows? Perhaps you will become the first man. Perhaps you are waiting to be Adam."

"Then you are—"

Again the dark surge of laughter. "I am the echo of a rib that has yet to sing."

"The rib is nowhere," said Mauris, drowsy with the effort of words. "It belongs to me, and I am unborn. Nowhere."

"Limbo," whispered the voice.

"Nowhere," mumbled Mauris.

"Limbo," insisted the voice.

"No . . . where," repeated Mauris weakly, fighting the cold fatigue of stillness, the weight of unbeing.

He could feel the laughter gathering, and knew that it would drown him. Desperation fought against the blind weariness sucking him into the heaving tide of sound. He tried to remember what it was like to pray.

"Oh, God," he whispered, "if I cannot die, let me become alive. Let there be light!"

Once more, the laughter struck. And the whirlpool opened.

There were no stars yet, but the light came like a pallid finger, probing the interior of the stricken ship. Captain Mauris looked about him at dim shapes; and the sensation of wonder grew, while fear plucked its familiar music from his taut nerves.

There was something wrong — desperately wrong. Suddenly, he understood. Everything had been reversed.

The copper cylinder, which had been bolted to the deck on the port side of the main control panel, now lay on the starboard side, its smooth fiery surface crumpled like paper. Below it, on the deck, lay beads of still liquid copper rain.

The starboard electrochron, with its numerals reversed,

now lay on the port side, above the gaping hole where the lightometer had been.

Captain Mauris turned his head to look at Kobler; but Phylo's berth now lay there in place of the physicist's. The captain knew without moving that his first officer was dead. Phylo stared at the deckhead, his features locked in a permanently vacant smile.

Glancing round at the S.F.P. chief, in Phylo's old place, Captain Mauris saw that Kobler's body was entirely relaxed. His eyes were closed; and in death, he had the appearance of one who is concentrating very hard. Judging from his expression, thought Mauris, he had been trying *in extremis* to discover his error.

The navigation deck of the *Santa-Maria* was a mausoleum — through the looking-glass. Everything — even, as Mauris discovered, the parting in his own hair — had been reversed. He knew, without feeling the necessity to confirm it by exploration, that he was the last man alive. The *Santa-Maria*, with the sole exception of its captain, was manned entirely by the dead.

"Poor devils," said Captain Mauris aloud. "Poor devils, they couldn't take the stillness. It made them too tired — dead tired!" The sound of his own voice, normal now, gave him a greater grasp on reality.

With ponderous, heavy movements, like a drunken man, he undid the straps of his contour-berth and struggled wearily to his feet. He went across to Kobler, feeling for his pulse with a forlorn hope.

"Dead tired," repeated Mauris slowly. He gazed ruefully at Kobler's pale face, set in a last frown of concentration. "*There are more things in heaven and earth, Horatio, than are dreamt of in your philosophy.*"

Mauris felt neither regret nor satisfaction. There was no joy in knowing that he had the final word, that Kobler would never laugh that one away.

Presently he pulled himself together, and made a cautious tour of the ship. He was as methodical as if it was a monthly routine inspection, and checked everything from the conditioner to the re-cycling plant. The ship, he noted ironically, was in perfect condition — but for two small details: the planetary and stellar drives were completely wrecked. Apart from the fact that the landing retard and auxiliary brake rockets were intact, the *Santa-Maria* was at the mercy of normal gravity fields.

There were only two reasonable possibilities. She might coast merrily in the void for ever, or drop eventually into a sun. The alternative was too improbable for consideration; for the chances of falling into the gravity field of an hospitable planet were several billion billion to one.

Finally, Captain Mauris was confronted with the task he had been subconsciously shirking. Steeling himself against a paralysing reluctance, he climbed up into the astrodome and looked at the stars.

He did not need star charts to tell him that this was not the home galaxy. As he gazed at the sharp, unfamiliar patterns, an already tight band seemed to constrict round his heart. Perhaps Kobler had succeeded. Perhaps the galaxy M 81 had been entered by a terrene ship for the first time. Much good it would do the United Space Corporation!

With a grim smile, Mauris recalled that final paragraph of the ship's articles. *If the Master should satisfy himself, and the authorised scientists concerned, that the danger factor is sufficient* . . . It was really very funny! Probably, sixteen hundred thousand light-years away, on a speck of cosmic dust, the *Field Testing Executive* had already set up their officious Court of Enquiry to consider possible reasons for the loss of their experimental ship.

Then suddenly he realised that if the *Santa-Maria* had indeed reached M 81, the planet Earth was not only sixteen hundred thousand light-years away, it was also sixteen hundred thousand years ago.

He had a sudden image of the *Field Testing Executive* with ape-like faces, sitting and jabbering pompously round a mud pool in some prehistoric steamy jungle. And Mauris laughed. He laughed loudly, raucously. He laughed until he cried — until weariness, in a sudden triumph, toppled him senseless on the deck. And there he lay, sleeping like a child whose nightmares materialise only when he is awake.

He never knew how long he slept. He was eventually wakened by a sharp agonising pain in his stomach. At last, through a fog of bewilderment, he diagnosed it as hunger. He staggered along to the mess-deck and operated the food delivery controls. A minute and a half later, he pulled a nicely roasted chicken, complete with potatoes and green peas, from the electronic cooker. He ate ravenously, and followed it up with cheese and biscuits, coffee and liqueur brandy. The brandy was a special bottle that had been optimistically saved for a celebration banquet. As he sipped it luxuriously, Captain Mauris thought of all the guests who were unable to attend. Gravely, he included Kobler, Phylo and all the rest of the *Santa-Maria's* personnel in the toast: "Absent friends!" Then he took the old corn-cob pipe from his pocket and lit up. Presently, Captain Mauris was feeling almost human.

He spent the rest of the 'day' launching dead bodies into space. Wearing his combination pressure suit, Captain Mauris lugged them one after another through the air-lock and gave them a shove. Kobler, Phylo and the rest went sailing smoothly out into the starry darkness. To each one, Captain Mauris gave a personal farewell, as if he might have been expecting an answer.

Presently, the *Santa-Maria* was surrounded by a slowly dispersing shoal of flying corpses whose presence was only inferred where they blotted out the background of unwinking stars.

Finally, when all that unwelcome furniture had been jettisoned, the captain went back to the navigation deck and made the ship accelerate for three seconds on her auxiliary rockets, thus leaving the shoal behind. Having accomplished this disagreeable task, Mauris felt much better.

But as he clambered into the astrodome for a further check on the unfamiliar star positions, it dawned on him that he had probably looked on a human face for the last time.

Nine 'days' later, by the ship's electrochron, Captain Mauris became convinced that he would not have to wait much longer. The star on the port bow had grown to the size of a penny. Presently, it would grow to the size of a football. Presently, the *Santa-Maria* and her captain would reach the end of their journey — in the purification of celestial fire.

He had already resigned himself calmly to his destiny and was, in truth, a little pleased that Fate had arranged a definite appointment with death for him. It was certainly preferable to drifting aimlessly for months, waiting until the food supply was exhausted, waiting until he went mad or plucked up enough courage to make the appointment on his own initiative.

The condemned man continued to eat hearty breakfasts, and settled down to enjoy, in his last days, what he had never yet experienced throughout his life — a period of sustained leisure. A period of rest and tranquillity, interrupted by nothing more serious than the push-button operations necessary for providing first-class meals.

Captain Mauris spent more and more time in the ship's library, projecting the micro-films of books he had never had the time to read. Intuitively, he went to the old writers, ranging at a leisurely pace through fiction and non-fiction, from Plato to Dickens, from Homer to H. G. Wells. He also browsed through the Bible, and amused himself by translating its profound convictions into the sort of language that Kobler used.

By the eighteenth day, Captain Mauris was confused, disappointed, excited and afraid. The now brilliantly blinding sun had changed its position from port bow to starboard quarter. Its place on the port bow had been taken by what seemed to be a green marble. Captain Mauris knew it was not another sun, and tried desperately not to allow himself to hope that it might be a habitable planet. Better to die by falling into an alien sun than survive, a castaway, on an unknown planet in some alien galaxy. His reason said so, but his emotions remained unconvinced.

It was then, for no reason at all, that he suddenly remembered the voice and the dreamlike laughter he had experienced in the total darkness, the absolute stillness of the galactic jump.

And Captain Mauris had a premonition.

On the twenty-fifth day the possibility became a certainty. The *Santa-Maria* was falling towards the green planet. There remained the problem of choice between two courses of action. Captain Mauris could either allow the ship to continue her free fall until she vaporised on hitting the atmosphere — if any — or exploded on ground impact; or else he could apply the auxiliary brake rockets and the landing retard, thus making a bid for survival.

The period of tranquillity was over: he was in a state of chronic indecision.

He was afraid in the very core of his being. He was afraid to make up his mind. The captain went uncertainly to the mess-deck, seeking consolation and enlighenment in the liqueur brandy. He did not find it.

Eventually, he was drawn back to the navigation deck as by a magnet. He climbed into the astrodome and regarded the green planet. It was expanding rapidly, almost visibly. With trembling fingers, Captain Mauris adjusted the manual telescope. He gazed through it at a startlingly close panorama of oceans, continents and islands. He stared hypnotically for a while, and felt the beads of cold moisture grow on his forehead.

At last he came down, and went to drink more brandy. It solved nothing, because he was still sober enough to face the choice.

Suddenly, he could stand it no more. He lurched unsteadily to the navigation deck, reached the control panel and threw in three switches almost simultaneously. Reflex-radar. altimeter and positioning gyro were immediately synchronised with the auto-pilot. Whether the reversed instruments functioned correctly or not, Mauris neither knew nor cared. He had rid himself of an intolerable weight. He had made a decision.

Immediately, he, who had accepted so much responsibility in his career, felt an overwhelming need to escape the responsibility of attempting to survive. He fled to the library and, forcing himself to try and forget the decision, placed a random micro-film in the book projector. It was *The Golden Ass* of Apuleius.

He looked at the words, and they had no meaning for him. He was too busy awaiting the shock of the first automatic blast of the auxiliary brake rockets.

After an eternity of hours that seemed years, he felt a sharp surge as the motors produced a field of double gravity, piling on the ship's own synthetic 1/3 G force.

Mauris fell sideways from his chair and lay on the bulkhead, groaning heavily. The rocket burst lasted five seconds, and he felt crushed by its relentless force. Abruptly, it ended: he slithered painfully to the deck.

Then the old habits reasserted themselves. The Master's place, in a power manoeuvre, was on the navigation deck. Captain Mauris picked himself up and made his way forward.

The second automatic power manoeuvre hit him before he could reach a contour-berth. A field of 5 G slammed him against the bulkhead of the navigation deck. He had fallen sideways about ten feet. He lay there spread-eagled, unconscious.

The auto-pilot had positioned the ship accurately. The ship's attitude, controlled by the gyro-manipulator, had brought the green planet dead astern; and with rockets blazing, the *Santa Maria* dropped backwards to that rapidly expanding surface. On the screens of the external visulators, the silvery shapes of mountains and hills, of rivers and forests leaped into a growing reality. The fleecy shapes of clouds passed like fantastic birds.

But Captain Mauris lay inert against the bulkhead; the accelerating G force crushing his unconscious body to the hard metal.

He awoke with every muscle aching from the tremendous stress of ordinary physical deceleration; but he awoke with a sensation of profound peace.

He picked himself up and climbed into the astrodome. The stars were no longer sharp unwinking points against a backcloth of jet. They twinkled, dancing to the whim of atmosphere.

Looking down, Captain Mauris felt his heart thump violently. The *Santa-Maria* had made a perfect automatic landing on what appeared, in the semi-darkness, to be smooth grassland. A few yards away, he thought he saw dimly the ripple of running water.

The United Space Corporation had laid down a cautious and definitive procedure for the exploration of strange planets. But, as Mauris told himself lightly, the United Space Corporation would not begin to exist even in its own galaxy for another sixteen hundred thousand years.

Casting discretion aside, Captain Mauris made his way aft

towards the air-lock. He seized a combination pressure suit and climbed into it impatiently. Then he entered the pressure chamber. He closed the door behind him and threw the switch. The needle remained steady, indicating that the external pressure — the planetary atmosphere — was at par.

Captain Mauris was surprised. He began to feel that it was part of some obliging dream. He pressed a luminous button on the bulkhead, and a heavy door of the entry-port swung open. The captain took a nylon ladder from its locker and secured one end to the stanchions of the entry-port. He tossed out the bundle of ladder and watched it drop through the misty atmosphere. Then slowly he climbed down.

Captain Mauris stood still and gazed at the terrain through a deceptive half-light. What he could see of it was so reassuringly normal as to be quite improbable. It might have been country in the temperate zones of Earth.

He tried to think of the fantastic chances against landing on such a planet after the *Santa-Maria* had crippled both her stellar and planetary drives in the extra-galactic jump. Logically, there was no chance. What had happened was merely impossible.

Luck, thought Captain Mauris. Or is it something else?

With sudden inexplicable determination, he tried to tempt Fate for the last time. He released the safety valve on his pressure suit. Nothing happened. With an audible laugh of triumph and amazement, he began to take off the headpiece. Presently he stepped out of the pressure suit, his oxygen cylinder unneeded.

Captain Mauris stood on an unknown planet and took in the unmistakable scents of summer. He felt drunk — drunk on the sheer fantasy of reality. As he gazed about him he saw, over a patch of woodland, grey streaks of light pushing back the darkness, dulling the stars. And fifty yards from the space-ship, he discerned the edge of a stream whose quiet murmur seemed suddenly to communicate with his awakened sense of hearing.

Giving a wild cry of pleasure, Mauris forgot all about space-frame physicists and the extra-galactic jump. He ran swiftly to the banks of the stream, knelt down and splashed the warm living water over his face. Then, impatiently, he tore off his stale clothes, and waded into the dark refreshing water.

And as he bathed, the intensity of light grew over the distant trees.

At last he came out of the stream, refreshed and exhilarated. He felt a warm breeze against his body, felt the blood coursing more rapidly through his veins.

He did not bother to dress, but walked wonderingly towards the increasing light.

The vault of darkness was being pushed slowly back, while the stars seemed to slip behind an invisible curtain.

Captain Mauris watched the landscape come quietly to life. Then he looked up at the sky.

"And darkness," said Captain Mauris, as he gazed at the fading stars, "darkness was upon the face of the deep."

He stood there, feeling the years roll back, feeling the vitality of youth drive back some secret winter. At length he turned round to look at the space-ship, to assure himself of the reality of the journey. There was nothing to be seen. The thin vein of water flowed quietly through vacant land.

Surprised at his own calmness, his lack of distress, he turned again towards the patch of trees. And from the direction that he would learn to call east, there rose the crimson edge of a new sun.

He remembered then and suddenly understood the message of a woman's voice in a dream of absolute stillness.

The Brain Child

THOUGH DR. THOMAS MERRINOE quietly deplored the fact that his ten-year-old son showed no sign of being a genius, he was thankful for small mercies. The boy did not possess two heads; nor was he a congenital idiot in the clinical sense. Objectively, it might almost be said that Timothy was a normal specimen, with, perhaps, a rather generous share of atavistic traits.

This was a source of continual wonder to Dr. Merrinoe. As the director of a team engaged in designing and building electronic brains, he was professionally shocked to think that even such an inferior calculator as a human being could be manufactured by unskilled labour. Fortunately or otherwise, this did not prevent him from begetting Timothy.

But as a fond father, Dr. Merrinoe fell somewhat short of the conventional standard. His wife, Mary, a sensible blonde who regarded trigonometry as a serious abdominal operation, had much difficulty in persuading him that babyhood and infancy were not only desirable but necessary. With characteristic impatience, Dr. Merrinoe had hoped to teach young Timothy chess at the age of three and differential calculus by four and a half.

After all, he argued, what was the use of science if it could not be applied to life? If it was possible to programme an electronic brain for all processes of mathematical reasoning, why could not the same thing be done to a small boy? He found the answer very quickly. It was tragically simple. In the matter of learning, the machine had no option: the boy had!

By the time he was ten, Timothy had not only managed to destroy Dr. Merrinoe's faith in every known method of education and driven him to seek consolation in bigger and better electronic brains, he had also managed to ignore the science of mathematics *in toto*.

Thus at the very apex of Dr. Merrinoe's career when, after three years of unremitting labour, he had brought to completion the electronic brain called Peeping Tom, the fruits of victory tasted slightly sour.

He had built a brain that could see, hear, speak and — in a limited sense — feel. He had built a brain that could make any other electronic bird-cage in the western world look foolish. He had programmed Peeping Tom to answer questions that nobody was clever enough to ask. Yet he could not teach his own son that half of a half was a quarter.

Sitting, one afternoon, in front of Peeping Tom's chromium-plated face, staring at his television-screen eyes and his loudspeaker mouth, Dr. Merrinoe felt no elation at all, only a faint bitterness. It was, he thought, a matter of regret that you could work out blueprints for practically everything except babies.

Recently, he had acquired the habit of talking to himself, fortunately, only when he was alone. But though his present reverie was no more than a quietly mumbled monologue, he was soon reminded that he was not quite alone.

"I beg your pardon, sir," boomed Peeping Tom, "but would you kindly state the precise terms of reference."

Dr. Merrinoe blushed guiltily, then remembered that Peeping Tom was only a machine, after all. "Go to blazes, you great glorified pianola! I wasn't talking to you."

"Sorry, sir," returned Peeping Tom abjectly, "but as there appears to be no one else present, and since you programmed me to tackle all questions, I concluded — "

"Switch yourself off," interrupted the physicist. "Go to sleep."

Peeping Tom's eyes glowed reproachfully. "Yes, sir."

"No, wait a minute!" snapped Merrinoe. "Are you intelligent?"

"No, sir. Merely clever."

"Correct. Now tell me who made you, who owns you and what you're worth."

"You designed me, sir, and your team constructed me. I'm owned by Imperial Electric Inc., who paid two million, two hundred and forty-five thousand, three hundred and sixty-seven dollars and thirty-three cents for materials and construction."

"That's right," agreed Dr. Merrinoe. "Can you beat me at chess?"

"Yes, sir."

"Can you calculate how many atoms there are in the cosmos?"

"Yes, sir — approximately."

"Can you work out how much rice the probable population of China will consume in 1975?"

"Yes, sir."

"Then," said Dr. Merrinoe with irony, "you will doubtless be able to solve a comparatively simple problem. Why does a baby suck its thumb?" He sat back complacently, waiting for Peeping Tom to admit defeat.

"A baby sucks its thumb," replied the brain unexpectedly, "for the following reasons: (a) because it is weaned too early, (b) because it is teething, (c) because it experiences insecurity, or (d) because it is hungry. If thumb-sucking persists, it is recommended that — "

"I'll be darned!" said Dr. Merrinoe. "Who programmed you with that stuff?"

Peeping Tom seemed to enjoy his moment of triumph. "You did, sir," he purred. "During the first test programming series, you arranged for me to store the contents of a thousand assorted handbooks in my memory banks. One of them was *Baby and Child Care* by Benjamin Spock, M.D."

Dr. Merrinoe was slightly furious. "Well then, you ampere-sucking incubus, perhaps you will kindly tell me why my son, Timothy, combines the physical characteristics of *Homo sapiens* with the mental ability of an anthropoid ape?"

"According to the Theory of Evolution," began Peeping Tom sententiously, "a primitive life-form is capable of— "

"Beating your dull-witted circuits out with a large spanner," interrupted the physicist, childishly indulging a much repressed desire to be rude. "Now allow me to re-phrase the question. Why is my son intellectually retarded, in spite of his general background?"

"May I request relevant data?"

"Proceed," said Dr. Merrinoe regally. "I will endeavour to be quite objective."

Despite his mechanical limitations, Peeping Tom contrived to give the impression of one drawing a deep breath. "I require to know his age, weight, height, physical type, shape of skull, approximate vocabulary, manual attainments, emotional characteristics, primary interests, habits, hobbies and ambitions. I also need to evaluate his relationship with his mother, and his relationship with you."

Dr. Merrinoe gazed at Peeping Tom's wall-length face, awestruck. "You don't want much, do you?"

"No, sir," agreed Peeping Tom blandly. Then he added: "If I may make a suggestion, sir, why not tell me about Timothy in your own way? I will marshal the relevant facts as they emerge."

Dr. Merrinoe was too immersed in the proposition to realise that a tremendous milestone in the history of electronic computers had just been passed. It was the first time one had ever made a suggestion on its own initiative.

"As I see it," began the physicist thoughtfully, "Timothy has one outstanding quality — stubbornness. He's as stubborn as a mule with a carrot complex. At first, I told myself it was only a sort of sturdy independence, but . . ." And he went on and on, talking through half the afternoon, confiding his problems to the machine of his own creation. Peeping Tom listened quietly, his square eyes dull with the deceptive somnolence of a fat cubist owl.

Finally, Dr. Merrinoe appeared to have exhausted himself. He broke off in the middle of a sentence whose point he had already forgotten, blinked foolishly, and came to the conclusion that he had recently been working too hard.

Peeping Tom seized the opportunity to deliver his verdict: "The available evidence, sir, points clearly to maladjustment. However, there is — "

"Maladjustment!" snorted Dr. Merrinoe. "Of course, the boy's maladjusted. That's what I've been wasting my time telling you."

Peeping Tom's eyes glowed brightly. "I do not infer that Timothy is a maladjusted child," he announced. "But you, sir, seem to be a maladjusted parent."

Dr. Merrinoe tried to preserve a tiny shred of scientific detachment. "An interesting theory," he conceded, with some irony. "Naturally, you have a solution to offer."

"Naturally," agreed Peeping Tom. "Since you have failed to arouse the boy's intellectual curiosity, it follows that a different stimulus should be applied."

"What?" enquired Dr. Merrinoe.

"Me," replied Peeping Tom.

Dr. Merrinoe closed the front door quietly behind him, and managed to raise a tired smile for his wife.

"Had a good day, darling?" asked Mary.

He noted with satisfaction that at thirty-seven, she was still uncommonly attractive. It was a great consolation.

"Terrible," he answered. "We've now got to the stage where the brain talks back. How about a nice, passionate kiss?"

"Make it eighty per cent nice and twenty per cent passionate," she said. "Dinner is in a critical condition."

He duly translated the wild impulse of abandon into a restrained domestic clinch.

"Where's Timothy?" he enquired casually.

"Watching some cloak-and-dagger stuff on the television."

Dr. Merrinoe made a noise like a punctured tyre. "I've a good mind to take an axe to that damned box of tricks. It's ruining his initiative, to say nothing of his critical faculty. When I was his age — "

"Darling," interrupted Mrs. Merrinoe gently, "you're using up too much adrenalin. I do wish you'd control your language a little more — at home, anyway. Little somethings have big ears."

"Humph! Has Wonder Boy dined?"

"Yes, he didn't want to miss the play."

"He didn't want to miss the play!" echoed Dr. Merrinoe irritably, following his wife into the dining-room. "Well, I suppose we ought to be thankful for a quiet meal together, anyway. Incidentally, I want to have a little chat with him afterwards. Do I smell something burning?"

Mary sighed. "Only yourself, dear. Look, why don't you see a psychiatrist?"

"About Timothy?"

"No, about you. Timothy's all right, but he seems to be giving you a king-size anxiety neurosis. If you left him alone, we'd all get along far better."

"Anxiety neurosis! The boy can't even tell me what the square root of eighty-one is without behaving like a contortionist."

"Neither can I."

Dr. Merrinoe tried to register a superior and at the same

time lecherous smile. "I didn't marry you for your brains, darling."

"And I," retorted his wife drily, "did not conceive Timothy for his. Now don't argue; it's bad for your digestion."

Dr. Merrinoe did not argue. He stared at the plate in front of him and brooded. It was all very well for Mary to dismiss the boy's intellectual weakness so lightly: those who have beauty do not usually concern themselves overmuch with brainpower. But while Mary's purpose in life was chiefly decorative, her son's definitely wasn't.

The trouble with Timothy, thought Dr. Merrinoe wearily, was that he didn't have very much of anything. His personality was nondescript; and though he certainly wasn't ugly, his features had a vague impression of being thrown together hurriedly, as if their creator had just been putting the finishing touches when the lunch whistle blew.

At last, when Dr. Merrinoe had simmered down and was lingering over his second cup of coffee and a cigarette, the object of this sad soliloquy deigned to put in his appearance.

"Hi, Dad," said Timothy, peering cautiously round the door.

"Hello, son," said Dr. Merrinoe, coaxing his face into what was meant to be a friendly smile.

Placing a more reasonable interpretation on the expression, Timothy advanced and tried to make his voice sound sympathetic: "Have you got neuralgia again?"

"No, I haven't got neuralgia," retorted his father irritably. "Whatever makes you think that?"

"Nothing."

"Then don't be an idiot. Did you enjoy the play?"

"It was passable. I wish they'd do another about space-flight, though."

"If you're interested in space-flight," began Dr. Merrinoe diplomatically, "how would you like to be able to work out the escape velocity of a moon rocket?"

"Not very much, thank you. I'd rather build one."

"You can't build one until you know enough maths to — "

Timothy yawned. "That's why I'd rather watch it on television."

His father began to look as if he'd got neuralgia again, only worse. "Timothy," said Dr. Merrinoe gently, "how would you like to come with me tomorrow and see Peeping Tom?"

"That old brain you've been throwing together?"

"Yes."

"Oh. Tomorrow's Saturday, isn't it?"

"It is. Does that make any difference?"

Timothy took a deep breath. "I was hoping to go to the movies."

Dr. Merrinoe likewise took a deep breath. "You're going to see the brain."

Mrs. Merrinoe gave her husband a glance of intense exasperation. It was a look that told him he would be in for a rough half-hour when Timothy had gone to bed.

On Saturday afternoon, a tall man and a small boy threaded their way through the vast weekend necropolis of Imperial Electric Inc. Dr. Merrinoe, with a mixture of curiosity and resignation, led Timothy, with a mixture of resignation and curiosity, among the coppery mass of spider-webs where Peeping Tom sat spinning his electronic dreams.

They climbed up a narrow staircase and entered the control room. Dr. Merrinoe pressed the master-switch, and Peeping Tom's eyes glowed drowsily. Timothy was mildly impressed.

"I am alert, sir," said Peeping Tom. "What are your instructions?"

Dr. Merrinoe settled Timothy in the audience chair.

"I shall leave my son, Timothy, here while I finish some work in my office. You will answer any questions he may ask, and generally keep him amused until I return."

"Yes, sir," boomed Peeping Tom.

Dr. Merrinoe could have sworn that the brain managed to wink. As he went downstairs again, he heard Timothy's opening gambit:

"If one and a half squirrels ate one and a half nuts in one and a half days, how may nuts would nine squirrels eat in nine days?"

"Eighty-one," murmured the physicist absently to himself, then shot a startled glance over his shoulder as he heard the brain say: "Fifty-four, sir."

For the next couple of hours, Dr. Merrinoe sat in his office and was entirely absorbed in a science-fiction pulp magazine. Eventually, he looked at the desk clock, and was suddenly jerked back from a world where amphibious octopods pursued beautiful earth-girls and almost caught them.

Two solid hours! He'd only meant to leave Timothy for forty-five minutes, or so!

Dr. Merrinoe hastily dropped the pulp magazine in his In Tray, then rushed out of the office and headed for the control room with some apprehension. It was all very well to let Peeping Tom attempt to improve Timothy; but what if Timothy had attempted to improve Peeping Tom?

As, with beating heart, he ran up the stairs, Dr. Merrinoe heard noises that sounded like the world's champion fast-talker limbering up in Chinese. But even as he opened the door, the screech slowed down until it became recognisable. A staccato volley marked the end of Peeping Tom's high pressure discourse. Timothy was fast asleep. Dr. Merrinoe felt a wave of relief.

"The experiment seems to have produced a negative result," he remarked, staring at his gently snoring son.

"Merely a deep level hypnosis, sir," explained Peeping Tom. "It was necessary to bypass the inhibiting factors before I could programme him adequately."

"Before you could *what*?" Dr. Merrinoe gaped.

"Before I could programme him adequately. He has now received an advanced course in mathematics and physics. I trust you will find the result satisfactory."

"There's just one small point," said Dr. Merrinoe, breathing heavily, "my son, you dim-witted squawk-box, is not a machine."

"No, sir," agreed Peeping Tom. "Therefore I allowed for a seventy per cent inefficiency. Perhaps you would care to waken him gently?"

The physicist did so. After a few moments, Timothy opened his eyes, yawned and stretched. "Very interesting," he remarked vaguely, "but can we go home now? I'm hungry."

Dr. Merrinoe treated the electronic brain to a pitying smile. But Peeping Tom made no comment, being, apparently, in a mood to hibernate.

The first reaction occurred after an unusually quiet tea. Instead of glueing himself to the television, Timothy disappeared into his father's study to emerge several minutes later with a book. He then found a quiet corner, settled himself and began to read.

"You've been bullying him," accused Mary in a whisper. "What went on this afternoon?"

"Nothing," said Dr. Merrinoe uncomfortably. "Nothing at all. I just left him to amuse himself with Peeping Tom while I cleared up some paperwork."

"Well, *somebody* has been bullying him," she insisted. "Or else he's feeling ill."

Timothy looked up from his novel. "Do you think a man could make himself invisible?" he asked.

"Certainly not," replied his father. "Why?"

"That's what this book is about — *The Invisible Man*. It looks a pretty good story."

Remembering his own H. G. Wells period, Dr. Merrinoe

was surprised. "Isn't it a little too hard for you, Timothy? *I* didn't read it until I was fourteen or so."

Timothy smiled. "It's old-fashioned, but I can manage. How would you like a game of chess, Dad? We haven't played for some time."

Dr. Merrinoe felt slightly uneasy. "I thought you didn't like chess. You used to say it bored you."

"It did," said Timothy blandly. "But I was younger then." He rubbed his freckled forehead, and looked puzzled for a moment. Then he went to a small bureau, took out the chess-men and board, and began to set up the pieces. He grinned pleasantly at his father.

"I think I'll watch the television," said Mrs. Merrinoe faintly, "while you two geniuses fight it out."

Dr. Merrinoe looked at her, gave a helpless shrug, then turned his attention to the chess board.

"Would you be angry if I beat you?" demanded Timothy.

"Certainly not," snapped Dr. Merrinoe, opening with the king's pawn. "I should be very glad indeed, also surprised."

"I shouldn't," said Timothy.

But after fifteen minutes, his father checkmated him easily, with a feeling of relief. The boy had not changed; or very little, anyway.

"You weren't playing your best," accused Timothy.

"I beat you, didn't I?"

A crafty smile flickered over Timothy's face. "Let's have another game. I'd forgotten some of the gambits."

"Thirsting for revenge?" said Dr. Merrinoe drily. He set up the pieces again.

Timothy frowned slightly, then said with some hesitation: "Would you give me fifteen dollars if I win?"

"What!"

"I said, would you give me fifteen dollars if I win?"

Dr. Merrinoe regarded his son gravely. "And what do I get if *I* win?"

"Thirty cents a week for a year," said Timothy promptly. "That's fair, isn't it?"

"I think so," answered his father, with a thin smile. "I hope this is going to be a lesson for you. Why do you want fifteen dollars?"

Timothy grinned. "I'll tell you after the game."

"Your move," said Dr. Merrinoe grimly.

It lasted slightly more than two hours, and proved to be quite a classic. At first, Dr. Merrinoe moved carelessly; then with more caution. After twenty minutes, he lost a knight and a bishop in rapid succession, while Timothy merely sacrificed three pawns.

This seemed to unnerve the physicist. He began to play with deathly concentration until a sudden stroke of brilliance, that should have given him the game, somehow cost him his queen.

Meanwhile, Timothy had taken to reading his novel between moves. Almost regretfully, he administered the *coup de grace*, at the same time reaching the end of Chapter Seventeen.

"Timothy," said Dr. Merrinoe in a cracked voice, as he reached for his billfold, "how did you do it?"

"Just followed the pattern," replied the boy enigmatically.

There was a profound silence while Timothy collected his winnings and, after a careful recount, pocketed the dollar bills. His father stared anxiously at this pint-size Frankenstein that was his own flesh and blood.

Eventually, Dr. Merrinoe was moved to consider the purpose behind this sinister confidence trick. "What are you going to do with the money?" he demanded.

"Buy a few things I need for some experiments."

"I see," said Dr. Merrinoe blindly.

Timothy yawned. "I think I'll go to bed now. Thanks for the games, Dad. I hope you didn't mind losing."

"Not at all," grated his father. "It was a pleasure."

Mrs. Merrinoe, whose interest in television had fallen to zero from the moment Timothy began to win, watched her small, retreating son with awe. She noticed that the copy of *The Invisible Man* was tucked firmly under his arm.

When he had closed the door behind him, she pounced on her husband like a broody lioness. "What's happened to my little boy?" she demanded. "What have you done to him?"

"Nothing — nothing at all," he said helplessly. "I expect Peeping Tom taught him a few tricks; but they'll soon wear off."

"Wear off!" snapped Mary. "I should hope so — for your sake! If that electronic egg-timer's done any harm to Timothy, I'll . . . I'll . . ." She froze him with an angry glare.

Remembering Peeping Tom's hypnotic programming, Dr. Merrinoe winced.

For the rest of the weekend, there was a somewhat uneasy armistice. Unconsciously, Dr. Merrinoe avoided his son as much as possible; while Timothy, for his part, spent a great deal of time in his own room.

The physicist discovered that a few more books had disappeared from his study, including one massive tome on wave mechanics. The thought of Timothy reading up on wave mechanics was no longer ridiculous: it was terrifying. But he made no comment, thinking it wiser to await results.

He did not have to wait long.

The storm broke on Monday evening. Returning home late after a long and unrewarding experiment, Dr. Merrinoe was confronted by a hysterical wife.

"Thank heaven you've arrived!" she sobbed. "I've been trying to call you for the last hour. You've got to do something about Timothy quickly, before I go out of my mind!"

"Timothy?" echoed Dr. Merrinoe nervously. "Where is he? Is he all right?"

At that moment, the dining-room door opened and a pair of

shoes walked down the hall. They were inhabited by an empty pair of stockings which invisibly supported a small boy's vacant suit.

"Hi, Dad," said Timothy cheerfully. "I wanted to give you a surprise."

Dr. Merrinoe cringed from the apparition. "Timothy," he croaked. "Timothy! What have you done?"

"Rearranged my molecular structure," replied Timothy calmly, "and lowered my refractive index to zero."

"It's — it's — it's impossible!"

"You said that before but, well, here I am. The man in the book did it, and so have I."

The sweat dripped from Dr. Merrinoe's forehead. "But Timothy, listen! The book was only a story — fiction. It just couldn't happen."

"It has," said Timothy. "Feel my hand." He prodded his father, not too gently, underneath the ribs. "Would you say that was fiction?"

Dr. Merrinoe coughed and sat down suddenly, his legs giving way like overloaded pit props. Mrs. Merrinoe, having now reached breaking point, fainted and with excellent timing slid gently into her husband's arms.

"Now see what you've done," he panted angrily. "We'd better get her on to the chesterfield." As he struggled with his wife's limp form, Dr. Merrinoe was helped by a pair of invisible hands.

He settled her in a relaxed position, then turned pathetically to the vacant suit. "How . . . how did you — "

"The apparatus is in my room," said Timothy. Anticipating his father's next move, he added: "No, don't go there. You may get electrocuted, or turn invisible or something. From now on, my room will have to be private."

Dr. Merrinoe was about to lay down the law, but thought better of it. "All right, son," he said meekly. "But Timothy, can you — can you change back?"

There was childish laughter. "I don't want to. This is fun. Besides, think what they'll say at school."

Dr. Merrinoe shuddered. He was thinking what the whole world would say. He was also thinking what the world might possibly *do*. At that moment, Mary opened her eyes. She looked as if she was getting ready to scream. It was the last straw. Dr. Merrinoe panicked.

"Timothy, you've got to change back," he pleaded. "You've *got* to. It's not decent. It's . . ." He floundered, inwardly praying for spiritual guidance. How could he ever hope to control an invisible boy?

Then suddenly Dr. Merrinoe was inspired. "I'll bet you twenty-five dollars," he said sadly, "that you can't become visible again."

"Done!" snapped Timothy. Suit, stockings and shoes galvanised into action. A door opened and slammed, and the invisible boy bounded upstairs three at a time. With an abject sigh, Dr. Merrinoe turned to his wife and patted her hand reassuringly.

"I'll divorce you," she hissed. "For extreme cruelty. You and that psychopathic brain!"

"Now, Mary," he soothed. "It's going to work out all right. We'll just have to watch him carefully for a while."

"Watch him carefully!" she stormed. "When at any moment he might decide to turn us into a couple of white mice."

"It's not as bad as that, dear. If you understood a little physics, I could — "

"Physics!" she scoffed. "Can *you* make yourself invisible?" She dabbed at her eyes with a handkerchief and sniffed. "It's the work of the Devil."

Unless the Devil had also been programmed by Peeping Tom, Dr. Merrinoe doubted if he would have enough scientific knowledge to be of practical assistance. But Mary was in no mood for reasonable discussion, so he let it pass.

He would have given anything to watch Timothy making himself visible again; but somehow that didn't seem advisable. He sat down and waited tensely.

A mysterious humming started upstairs. It sounded like a muffled hornet. Presently, it changed into a high-pitched whirring that died slowly into silence. Then there was a sound like breaking glass.

A few moments later, Timothy came back into the room, wearing a benign smile on his chubby, substantial face.

Dr. Merrinoe mopped his forehead. Then he saw the purposeful gleam in Timothy's eye, and hastily took out his billfold. He selected a five and two tens.

"Now, Timothy," he waved them slowly in front of the boy's nose, "I want you to promise that you'll never make anyone or anything invisible with that — apparatus. In fact, it would be a good thing if we took it to pieces tonight. Of course, I'll just take a few notes for the sake of a scientific record, but — "

"Nobody goes into my room," interrupted Timothy decisively. His hand closed round the bills. "Now that I've done it once, I'm beginning to lose interest. I only worked on it because you said it was impossible. But I've just discovered a far more interesting problem."

"What's that?" squeaked Dr. Merrinoe in top falsetto.

"Anti-gravity," said Timothy with a happy smile.

Dr. Merrinoe experienced an odd darkness descending. The room began to sway slightly; and he had a vague feeling that presently the floor would rise up and hit him.

From far, far away, he heard Timothy eagerly explaining why the General Theory of Relativity was just a little unsound. But Dr. Merrinoe was more concerned with the practical side. He was already figuring how much it would cost him *not* to go to the moon.

Welcome Home

The United Nations ship swooped low like a kingfisher over the vast desert, then rose suddenly in a bright arc of ascent as if she had decided that Mars was not worth exploring anyway. But at ten thousand metres the swift climb died into a moment of motionless beauty; and she sat lightly on a tail of green flame, suspended between stars and destination, until imperceptibly the flame shortened and she sank gently towards the arid waste.

Touchdown was smooth and undramatic. So smooth that it might have been the hundredth touchdown of a regular interplanetary ship handled by a bored and seasoned crew. As it happened, however, this was an occasion — one that would eventually become a date in a history book to plague the memory of small boys — for neither the United Nations ship nor any other terrestrial vehicle had visited the Red Planet before. And her crew were the first human beings to venture further than the moon.

They were, however, all fairly experienced space travellers. Colonel Maxim Krenin, the director of the expedition and pilot of the *Pax Mundi*, had made the Earth-moon shoot five times. He had also made more than a score of lunar test shoots. So had Commander Howard Thrace, the navigator. And besides providing a very notable example of Russo-American technical co-operation, these two were firm personal friends.

The remaining three members of the expedition, Professor Bernard Thompson, representing Britain, Professor Yves Frontenac, representing France, and Dr. Chan S. Chee, representing China, had each logged at least three major shoots and an impressive number of satellite-orbit hours. During the long fall to Mars, they had had ample time to shake down as a team and to work out their exploration strategy in detail.

And now here they were in their slender titanium hull, poised like a classic monument on the equatorial Martian desert. Radiac tests had been made, the ground-level atmosphere had been analysed, and the first Earthmen were about to set foot on the sands of Mars — symbolically, perhaps, at high noon.

Even before they stepped outside the ship, they already knew enough about Mars to be slightly humiliated by their own previous theories and the general opinion of scientists on Earth.

For decades, terrestrial astronomers had assured everyone that Mars was virtually inimical to life, despite an insistent popular belief in grotesque and complex life forms and even Martian intelligence.

Mars, claimed the astronomers with all the authority of men capable of making powerful deductions on the most slender evidence, was a planet almost without oxygen, water or warmth. The so-called canals were not canals at all but a series of flux fissures entirely geological in origin. And they went on to predict that, because of the climate, the most highly developed forms of life that could be expected would be similar to lichen, perhaps, or simple cacti.

These, roughly, had been the general views of the U.N. expedition — until their arrival. But even before touchdown, while they were orbiting at a hundred thousand metres, they were able to discern among other things that the canals were in fact, or had been, canals, and that the atmosphere contained even enough oxygen to support human life if not comfortably, at least bearably.

Then, when they went into low level orbit, they made a discovery that seemed to eclipse everything else — except perhaps the canals — in significance.

They saw pyramids: ten tremendous Martian pyramids spaced at great distances from each other over the comparatively featureless plains and naked deserts. The discovery was more than a discovery: it was a revelation. And the revelation had more significance, more far-reaching implications, than any other discovery in the entire history of man.

More than four centuries previously an obscure Polish astronomer, Nicolaus Copernicus, had shocked the world by his assertion that Earth was not uniquely fixed at the centre of the cosmos. But eventually both theology and pride had recovered from the blow. For, though Earth itself could no longer be regarded as unique in size, position or significance, its master race, *Homo sapiens*, was still the chosen of God. Nowhere else, it was held, could there be creatures of such intelligence and inventiveness, able to be used as divine instruments in the eternal battle between good and evil. So said the priests and the philosophers and all who contributed to the cult of human significance.

And for four hundred years, the proposition of the uniqueness of man was not seriously challenged.

But now?

The news of the Martian pyramids had already been beamed to Lunar City and Earth before the U.N. ship touched down. And back had come a definitive order to abandon for the time being the orderly sequence of scientific exploration and concentrate upon the pyramids. The expedition to Mars was, in financial terms, an extremely costly venture; and as, in the end, it would be the ordinary citizens who would have to foot the bill, here was a chance to give them something truly spectacular for their money.

The order did not cause disappointment at all among the U.N. team. The mystery of the pyramids was hypnotic in a way that no previous space discovery had ever been. Somehow the existence of structures designed and built by intelligent beings established an atmosphere of contact and communication which considerably diminished the heavy mood of loneliness that had built up on the long shoot to Mars. It was as if Mars had expected the *Pax Mundi*, as if the pyramids were a kind of gigantic planetary greeting.

The nearest one now lay some three kilometres to the north of the U.N. ship, its smooth black symmetry rising almost half a kilometre from the desert. As Colonel Krenin came out of the airlock, glanced momentarily at the impressive shape and then made his way down the nylon ladder, his feeling of awe seemed to expand like a great inward bubble.

Then suddenly the historic moment was over before he was aware of it. He had already set foot on the sands of Mars. After him came Commander Thrace and the rest. None of them said anything for nearly three minutes. They just stood and stared.

Presently, the honour of uttering the first terrestrial words on the planet fell to Professor Thompson. He gazed at the pyramid, sighed deeply, and in modern Lingua Franca, said: "At this very moment, more than anything, I want a cigarette."

"Why not?" remarked Dr. Chee blandly. "The oxygen content of the air is rich enough. But I do not think your cigarette will taste quite the same."

"Have a Gauloise," said Professor Frontenac.

"Have a Stuyvesant," said Commander Thrace.

The Englishman frowned slightly, felt in his own pocket, then accepted a French cigarette.

"You're right," he remarked after a few moments. "They taste quite different."

"Gentlemen," said Colonel Krenin, "a formal speech will be required for transmission to Earth, and since my Lingua

Franca is less proficient than it might be . . ." He took a miniature recorder from his shoulder bag and looked at his companions hopefully.

Professor Frontenac smiled. "The pyramids are probably the remains of a civilisation that was ancient even when terrestrial man was still a creature of the caves and forests. Among us, Dr. Chee represents one of the oldest terrestrial civilisations . . . I think perhaps it is fitting . . ."

Dr. Chee bowed, then made a brief speech for the benefit of Krenin's recorder, the waiting millions on Earth and, perhaps, solar posterity. He spoke of the wonder of the journey, the even greater wonder of discovery and the solemnity of touchdown. But even Dr. Chee's restrained language and abstract nouns could not avoid contamination by the boyish excitement and impatience that suddenly gripped the U.N. team.

While he was still talking, Commander Thrace ran back up the nylon ladder and swung the light electric derrick out from the ship's lower entry-port. Then he and Professor Frontenac began to lower sections of the six-seater hiduminium monowheel they had brought. Soon the others were assembling it; and in less than half an hour the twenty-foot diameter transport wheel was operational with its gyro-stabiliser purring evenly.

Professor Thompson shaded his eyes and gazed at the pyramid, massive and sombre under the bright Martian sun. "Perhaps we should eat something before we venture on any exploration," he suggested without much conviction.

"Do you feel like eating?" enquired Dr. Chee.

"No, but I thought — "

"I will bring some emergency packs," called Colonel Krenin from the ship's open airlock. "If necessary, we can dine at the pyramid."

Commander Thrace had been staring fixedly at what appeared to be a large rounded boulder, some fifty centimetres high, which lay a few metres from the base of the ship.

"Anybody notice this before?" he asked.

No one could remember seeing it.

"Look," said the commander. "Look closely."

The boulder was moving very slowly over the dull red sand. They watched it move across what looked like a tiny patch of moss; but when the boulder had passed, the plant was no longer to be seen.

Frontenac went up to the boulder and touched it. Then he tapped it. There was a look of ecstatic mystification on his face.

"Let's turn it over," suggested Thrace.

They did so. The face of the underside was soft. It seemed like a compound of sponge and snail. Very slowly it began to withdraw into the security of its thick protective shell.

"Marvellous, superb, exquisite!" exclaimed Frontenac, lapsing into his native French. "What a beautiful animal!"

"Or plant," added Thompson drily.

"Animal," insisted the Frenchman. "By all the laws —"

"On Mars," interrupted Thompson, "the definitions we have been accustomed to use may not necessarily apply."

Gently they replaced the 'boulder' face down on the sand.

"Now we must go to the pyramid," said Colonel Krenin. "Earth will want our first report quickly. I have put the still, cine and telecameras in the monowheel. Do each of you carry crew radios and personal recorders?"

They nodded.

"What of my specimen?" said Frontenac. "I wish to observe it."

"Then you will also observe the ship," said Krenin, smiling. "Someone should stay."

The Frenchman wore the look of one who wished mightily to be in two places at once.

After a final check-over, the rest of the expedition climbed aboard the monowheel, with Commander Thrace taking the control stick. As they set off towards the pyramid, they saw Professor Frontenac kneel down and put his head close to the sand. He was trying to see how his pet 'boulder' managed to move.

The desert was, for the most part, surprisingly smooth; and the journey to the pyramid took barely ten minutes. On the way they passed several small varieties of plant and one curious patch of tall grass that contrived to strike with whip-like force at the monowheel as it went by. They also passed several of the 'boulder' creatures which Professor Thompson temporarily called Frontenac's Friends.

As they neared the base of the great pyramid, their sense of excitement became so intense that it seemed to fuse into an unnatural calm. They were drunk with wonder. They felt like sleep-walkers who were yet wide awake.

The structure not only dominated the landscape, it seemed to reach the very zenith of the sky. Compared to this, the pyramids of Egypt were as the toys of a child.

First of all they drove slowly round the whole edifice in the monowheel, just gazing at it, unable to find either adequate comment or adequate explanation. It seemed quite beyond explanation — beyond possibility even. Yet there it stood: the greatest monument ever presented to the sight of man.

Its face appeared to be constructed of layer upon layer of a kind of black basalt, each single slab of which, though worn perhaps by sandstorm and blizzard, was still flawless in its dimensions. The layers rose inward like a triangulated giant's stairway, reaching towards the shimmering apex that was itself a stepping-stone to the sky.

But in the centre of each of the massive steps, there was a shiny whitish slab veined with gold and crimson and green and silver — iridescent as a crystal mirror, more beautiful than any known marble of Earth.

The first of these slabs, like the layer of basalt in which it was set, lay half covered by the dull red Martian sand. The four men climbed out of the monowheel and gazed at it; and as they did so, the slab immediately above swung noiselessly back, revealing a faintly luminous passage. Out of this a long, light metal gangway extended itself with equal silence, its protruding end being lowered slowly to the level of the sand more than two metres below.

The end of the gangway came to rest almost at Colonel Krenin's feet.

"By all the saints!" murmured Professor Thompson hoarsely. "It knows we're here!"

Commander Thrace was the first to recover himself. "Photo-electric equipment," he suggested helpfully. "Or maybe vibration sensors."

"The point is," said the colonel, "do we accept the invitation or not?"

Dr. Chee smiled. "At least it has been put to us very gracefully."

"It could be some kind of trap," remarked Commander Thrace.

Krenin frowned. "Too elaborate. We could have been dealt with more efficiently and economically."

Professor Thompson smiled. "Will you walk into my parlour, said the spider to the fly."

"Some parlour," said Thrace.

"It could be an intelligent spider," retorted the Englishman.

Dr. Chee raised his eyebrows slightly. "One can hardly appreciate the psychology of a race capable of constructing pyramids to trap space travellers," he ventured drily.

Colonel Krenin became practical. "Two of us will accept the invitation," he said, "and two will remain here."

"We'll draw lots," said the commander. He took four cigarettes from his pack, tore the filter tips from two of them and put them behind his back. When he displayed his hand once more, four smooth cigarette ends were showing. "The two short ones stay."

Colonel Krenin drew first and got a full cigarette. Both Thompson and Chee drew short ones.

"We will limit ourselves to a maximum of one hour," said the colonel. "We will make radio contact only in an emergency. On no account are you to follow." He tested the gangway with his foot.

"Good luck," said the professor.

"You already have too much of it," grumbled Dr. Chee.

With Krenin leading, the two men went cautiously up the gangway. At the top, they turned to look at their companions for a moment, then entered the passage.

The inside walls were faced with the same kind of stone as the slab that had swung back to reveal the entrance. It glowed greenly, providing a pleasant and restful light by which the two men were able to see their way ahead. After a brief hesitation, they walked resolutely forward.

The passage proceeded in a straight line, sloping slightly downwards, and looked as if it must lead to the centre of the pyramid's base. If that were so, Krenin and Thrace were in for quite a long walk.

At first they advanced slowly and in silence as if they half expected a pit to open suddenly at their feet, or some other equally noxious trick. But there were no tricks, and after a few minutes they gained enough confidence to walk forward at a brisk pace. After a time, they turned round and looked back. The opening was still visible as a tiny point of light, but it already seemed several kilometres away.

"The plot thickens," said Commander Thrace softly to himself in English.

"I beg your pardon?" said Colonel Krenin in Lingua Franca.

"Sorry. The situation is absolutely baffling."

"Not absolutely," remarked Krenin with a thin smile.

"There is much to indicate order, intelligence and purpose."

Suddenly, Thrace grabbed his companion's arm and pointed to the wall just ahead. A rectangular slab of black stone had been let into it, and on the stone a diagram had been engraved.

It was a symbolic representation of the solar system. All the planets but two were shown simply as circles on lines indicating their orbital paths. But the third planet, Earth, was represented by a brilliant green stone; and the fourth planet, Mars, by an even more brilliant red one.

Krenin and Thrace were more than amazed: they were dumbfounded.

After a few moments, Commander Thrace broke the spell. "We'd better press on," he said. "We have only forty-five minutes left, and I have a feeling there are more and bigger surprises waiting for us."

He was right.

After a few more steps, they discovered another black slab let into the wall. This one showed the symbols for an atom of hydrogen, one of oxygen and one of carbon. The two men stared at it in silence and then passed on. Words seemed totally inadequate.

The next slab they encountered showed what seemed to be a representation of a simple protein molecule. After that came what looked like the molecular pattern of desoxyribonucleic acid. And after that came the greatest shock of all.

There were two parallel slabs, one on each side of the passage. They showed with brilliant anatomical detail two human beings — a man and a woman. Both were represented, however, without any hair.

"I will now believe anything," said Commander Thrace in a shaky voice. "Anything at all."

"Then — then man is not a unique product of Earth!" exclaimed the colonel. "Or perhaps . . ." The thought was too fantastic to be expressed.

With an effort, Thrace managed to rouse himself from the subtle state of hypnosis into which the diagrams seemed to be drawing him. "We ought to keep moving," he said reluctantly.

Krenin glanced at his own wristwatch and sighed. "There is so much, so much to observe, to consider."

They continued on their way along the greenly glowing passage, feeling like children trapped in a mysterious dream world that was somehow confused with reality. Presently, they came to a sharp turn in the passage; and as they negotiated it they were presented with the most fantastic sight of all.

Suddenly, they found themselves in a vault large enough to contain any of the great cathedrals of Earth. It was suffused with the same green glow as the passage, but deeper now so that, for a moment, the two men felt as if they were walking across the floor of a great subterranean ocean.

Then the oceanic feeling gave way to lofty revelation — a feeling of infinite space and infinite beauty. It was as if they were engulfed by a cloud of soundless music blown all about them by dark draughts of light.

For a bright suspended moment, the two men felt as if they were dying. And then as if they were instantly reborn.

The walls of the vault were alive with solid pictures, fading and merging and blooming in a magnificent visual symphony. Here, for a moment, they glimpsed in all its awful grandeur the birth of the solar system. The fiery wisps of planets were flung out from a ravaged solar womb, out into the dark immensities of space. The wisps condensed into burning droplets, the droplets into solid spheres. And then the vision dissolved into a pattern of lifeless oceans, of monstrous volcanoes and blinding rivers of rock; of explosion and cataclysm and deluge; of floating continental islands and desperate aeons of scalding rain.

Again the patterned pictures changed . . .

They peered deep into the heart of the angry seas, witnessing the emergence of life itself. They saw the life and death of a myriad lowly creatures; the fantastic centuries of slaughter caused by the receding waters; the inevitable, blind, courageous conquest of the land.

They saw forest and desert, ice-cap and tundra. They saw the great reptiles locked in titanic combat through their flickering sovereignty. They glimpsed monstrous leathery wings that seemed to sprout brilliant feathers in a single moment, transforming saw-toothed killers into veritable birds of paradise. They saw shaggy and ravenous beasts of the trees miraculously walking upright, seeking the tools and tribal unity that would lift their restless minds above and beyond the hungry, all-consuming darkness of prehistory.

They saw the birth of civilisation, cities blossoming like strange stone flowers on plains and in valleys. They saw death and discovery, warfare and worship; plague, fire, flood and famine. They witnessed the endless conflict of man against nature, the vital tragedy of man against man. The age of glory and the age of machines. And also the age of destruction, when darkness fell from the air.

Then suddenly the walls of the vault clouded and became clear. The visual saga of creation dissolved into the depths of a green eternity.

And then there was a voice. The voice came from nowhere and yet it was everywhere, rolling through the vault like thunder, whispering like the wind through summer grass. It was neither the voice of a man nor a woman. It was simply a voice.

"To the living of the third planet from the dead of the fourth planet, greetings," said the voice. "To the star children from the star children, greetings.

"This, our salute to you, bridges fifty thousand planetary journeys round the star that is our sun. But let these words be to you more than the echo of distant ghosts, for there is that which binds the third and fourth planets inseparably.

"In the pyramids we have built we bequeath to you the only possible gift — the story of our race. Once we of the fourth planet lived on a green and pleasant world. We were a race of leisure and wealth and power, having tamed for our needs the energies of the elements and the fantastic energies of the sun. We have even probed the secrets of life itself, so that immortality was ours. But you have seen the ultimate achievement of our greatness: it is nothing more than the barren desert and the pyramids in which our memory yet endures.

"It is true that we gained immortality; but the price we paid was too high for, in the end, we became almost totally sterile. It is true also that we had at our command unlimited physical power. But our spiritual power was unequal to the challenge; and in quarrel over philosophies whose very defence by force indicated their weakness, we succeeded eventually in destroying both our race and the living richness of our planetary home. We had conquered the forces of nature, but we were defeated by the forces in our own hearts.

"Before all was lost, however, and in a brief period of sanity, we gathered together the few young and fertile people remaining to us. Determining that our race should not perish entirely in vain, we built transports to bridge the gap between the planets. And then our most precious possessions — our children — were carried to your world, their minds cleansed of the bleak wisdom and sophistication that had been our downfall.

"There, in the forests of the third planet, we left them to endure all the slow anguish and adventure of a new spiritual and physical development in a new unsullied world.

"You who hear these words are their and our descendants. You have made yourselves the masters of unlimited physical power once more. We pray that, this time, your racial spirit, reforged in the fires of evolution, will prove equal to the challenge.

"We pray, also, that you will take this, the fourth planet, and, in harmony of effort and unity of purpose, use your skills and energies to restore to it the green fertility that flourished long ago. You are truly our children and our future. Welcome Home."

There was silence and stillness. The two men looked at each other. The thoughts and feelings that possessed them were far beyond the scope of words. Presently, they knelt down for a few moments as if the vault itself had become a temple, as if their quiet thanksgiving would somehow be heard. Then at last they turned back to the passage, slowly retracing their steps . . .

Colonel Krenin and Commander Thrace were ten minutes overdue when they emerged from the pyramid.

Dr. Chee and Professor Thompson were set to explode their recent anxiety and present curiosity in a great blast of questions; but when they saw the expressions on the faces of the two silent men, all the questions died.

"We found the Answer," said Commander Thrace at length.

"What answer?" asked Dr. Chee gently. His companions were so abnormally calm that they seemed to be suffering from shock.

"There is only one Answer," said Colonel Krenin. "It is your turn now. Go, and you too will find it."

"There is no hazard?" asked Professor Thompson.

Colonel Krenin smiled. He seemed to be gazing at something many millions of miles away or, perhaps, many thousands of years ago. "Only to our pride," answered the colonel softly.

Thompson and Chee could make nothing of that; and as there was only one obvious thing to do, they too entered the passage, leaving the colonel and the commander to wait for them.

Presently, Commander Thrace said: "I have just remembered something. How could you possibly understand the Voice? He — it was speaking in English."

The colonel shook his head. "No, Russian."

The commander thought for a moment. "Neither Russian nor English," he said. Then he added: "After that, I think we shall never be quite the same men again."

Colonel Krenin gazed out over the bleak Martian desert. "No, never the same," he agreed. "Soon it will be Professor Frontenac's turn; and after that we must set up the cameras and television relays. Then all the different peoples of Earth will never be the same again."

Commander Thrace idly stirred the dry red sand with his feet. He made miniature mountains and valleys, and absently began to visualise a tiny network of roads.

At length he said: "Do you think we shall ever manage to reclaim this wilderness?"

"We have to," said Colonel Krenin simply. "This is home."

Judgment Day

I AM AN old man now, but the memory of that September morning fifty years ago has burned into my brain so that, day or night, the scene is still alive for me with all the terrible reality of a nightmare. I shall not be sorry to die because then the memory, too, will die. And for me that is the only possible meaning of peace.

Sometimes I realise that it is very pleasant here on the farm in this Derbyshire valley. Especially in spring when I have finished the morning stint of weaving and can look forward to spending a long, lazy afternoon sitting in the doorway of my cottage. There is nothing to do then but watch the sunlight slanting over low blue-green hills and listen to the voices of the children at play. And wait until darkness falls . . .

They are a strange breed, these children of the Dark Age. Their blue eyes are filled with longing and their thoughts are centred not upon the future but on what they regard as the glorious past. The age of heroes, the almost mythical age of powered machines and teeming cities, radio and television, jet craft and fast cars.

And on clear evenings there are still satellites passing across the sky like bright stars in hurried transit. A few nights ago one of them fell out of orbit and passed through the upper atmosphere, a thin curved shaft of radiance, until the friction made it explode into a tiny flower of light. And so, perhaps, they will all eventually come down, one by one, until there is nothing left to show that man was once at the very gateway to the stars.

The children like to hear about the satellites. But I think they do not quite believe in them. Or, at least, not in the way that I do. As a survivor of the age in which satellites were fired into orbit, I can recognise them for what they are, engines of destruction, awaiting the signal to release their bombs from a button that is no longer there to be pushed. Though some of them — the first ones — are no more than tiny celestial laboratories, perhaps still sending their faint bleep-bleeps down to a deaf world . . .

For the children, however, the satellites are simply mobile stars, impressive only because they were sent upon their lonely journeys by the Great Ones.

The Great Ones!

It is sad to think that an entire mythology can grow in the space of a single lifetime. Human beings do not seem to be able to live without myths: and perhaps, after all, the myths created from an already shadowy past are merely clouded mirror images of hope for the future. Perhaps the children are creating for themselves some kind of challenge, an ideal that will carry them through this Dark Age into a world where progress will have a clearer objective than racial suicide.

Yet, whenever I hear them talk of the Great Ones, I find it hard to suppress a surge of bitter inward laughter. Somehow I manage to keep silent, for it is unwise to disillusion the young. But I cannot help thinking that now there are probably less than ten million people on a planet that once supported nearly four thousand million. And that, to me, is a fitting epitaph for the Great Ones . . .

I remember them as men, ordinary men in an extraordinary world of their own making. Men with fast brains and slow hearts; with the gift of creation in their dreams and the impulse of destruction in their fingers.

Most of all, I remember that bright September morning when civilisation died; and the few terrible days that followed when it seemed as if the human race could no longer survive.

It was a crisp and beautiful morning, with sunlight spreading a gold patina over fields and hills and cities; and with all the strange, exhilarating scents of early autumn drifting lazily across the still air.

I had just been discharged from hospital after a minor operation. And, to me, the world was doubly attractive because, after spending two weeks in the restricted cosmos of a general ward, I felt as if I were seeing it for the first time.

Justine, my wife, had come to meet me. We were both especially pleased because I had been discharged in time to celebrate her twenty-fifth birthday. She had a taxi ready to take me home and I remember how we quarrelled a little even while we were kissing each other, because I wanted to walk through the park and she was convinced that the effort would exhaust me. Eventually I won my point. The morning was too lovely for us to waste any of it riding in a taxi; and we set off arm in arm, walking very slowly because my muscles were still stiff; and although the incision had healed remarkably well, my stomach was still very tender.

After twenty minutes we reached the park. By then the exertion of being upright was beginning to tell on me, so we found a bench where I could sit down and rest for a few minutes. We were not the only ones to be taking advantage of the sunshine. Here and there babies and small children were romping about, watched indulgently by their mothers, while on the other benches a few old people basked with half-closed eyes as if they had all the time in the world before them.

About two hundred yards away, I noticed a small group of people standing in the middle of the carriageway. They looked as if they were gazing at something on the ground, but

I didn't pay much attention until I saw a figure detach itself from the group and run quickly towards the far end of the park. Somewhere in the distance we heard the incongruously frenzied ring of an ambulance bell.

"There must have been an accident," said Justine. "Do you think I ought to — "

"No, darling," I said. "Stay here and look after your own invalid. There are enough people about, and I suppose they've done what's necessary."

The ambulance had already turned into the broad carriageway at the other end of the park.

"I should hate to have to go into hospital on a morning like this," murmured Justine as she watched the ambulance heading towards the little group.

"Hear, hear," I agreed with some feeling. "Maybe it's not very serious. I expect some dear old soul has slipped on a banana skin, or something like that."

But even as I spoke the subtle ordinariness of that lazy autumn morning was crushed like a rose beneath some invisible foot. Suddenly the ambulance swerved from the carriageway and lurched drunkenly across the grass towards a large oak tree. The thud of impact rolled dully through the still air.

"My God! What the hell — " I stopped. A small child — a girl of about seven — who had been playing near our bench suddenly began to scream. But the scream was terminated abruptly by a spasm of projectile vomiting. Her whole body convulsed as the contents of her stomach were thrown up in a thin, pathetic stream.

Justine jumped to her feet and ran towards the child. But she had taken no more than half a dozen steps before the little girl crumpled at the knees and fell on to the grass, her tiny body still shaken by that terrible retching.

By the time I had managed to get to my feet and walk gingerly to where Justine was kneeling by the child, the convulsion had subsided into a peculiar twitching. Justine was loosening the little girl's frock which seemed to be rather tight. I tried to kneel down and help her; but there was a sudden stab of pain in my operation scar, and I couldn't.

I just looked down helplessly at the now unconscious child. Mucus was trickling slowly from her nose and out of the corner of her mouth. Justine had loosened the clothing and was cradling the little girl in her arms. Occasionally there was a deep sigh and then half a moan as if the child were simply asleep and troubled by nightmares.

"What is it, darling?" asked Justine, gazing at me anxiously. "We shall have to get some help, shan't we?"

I was about to reassure her that it was probably just a nasty spot of tummy trouble when I remembered the ambulance and glanced vaguely across the park to see what was happening. The words died on my lips.

About forty yards away an old man was being sick. The way he heaved almost made me think I could hear his gasping. A little beyond him a youngish woman had fallen from one of the park benches and lay on the ground, her limbs contorting as if she had suddenly become a victim of some kind of epileptic fit.

Farther away, there was a young mother running towards a child who was trying to scream and be sick at the same time. But after eight or nine steps she, too, collapsed and became helpless in the grip of her own spasms.

It was happening everywhere. With terrifying abruptness, the park had begun to look like a nightmarish battleground where an invisible enemy struck quickly and at random. A few minutes ago there had been nothing more important to do than sit on a bench and bask in the warm serenity of an early autumn day. But now . . .

Now I thought that perhaps I was mad. There was a terrible sound in my ears, which for a second or two, I refused to recognise. It was strangely low, yet piercing, and seemed to come not only from the park but from the entire city beyond. It was the sound of people . . .

Justine's eyes were wide with horror. I wanted to give her some comfort or reassurance, but I had none to give.

"Oh, darling!" she cried. "*What's happening*?"

I could only look at her helplessly. The weakness I had felt after coming out of hospital seemed to be rolling over me in waves.

Then the child stirred. She opened her eyes and glanced at Justine with a puzzled expression. "Where is Mummy? I'm hurting. I want — " She began to sob.

"Mummy is coming," said Justine. "She won't be long now. We'll just look after you until — "

But suddenly Justine was flung over backwards as the pathetic little body became racked with convulsions. The whole frenzied attack could not have lasted more than half a minute. Then the convulsions gave way to a harsh dry coughing. The child's fingers burrowed into the earth until she was clutching tiny handfuls of soil and grass. I could not bear to see the expression on her face.

"We've got to get away from here," I said desperately. "It's like some damned plague spot. There must be somewhere that — "

"I'm not going to leave her," said Justine flatly. She had picked herself up and was now kneeling by the child who lay curled up on the grass like a tired baby. "I *can't* leave her." Futilely she began to stroke the small curved back and murmur meaningless, soothing words.

"We can't do anything," I pointed out wearily. The effort of trying to cope with things I could not understand was becoming too much. When I left hospital, despite all the warnings, I had not realised how weak I still was. But now I felt as if I were being put through some kind of endurance test, and I knew that I couldn't last the course.

"Darling, you look terrible," said Justine. "Sit down a few moments while I try and get to a telephone."

Somehow, I knew that getting to a telephone was just a waste of time. There would be a lot of people trying to get to telephones — and a lot of telephones that would never be answered.

"We're not leaving each other," I panted, as she helped me to lower myself to the grass. "Whatever happens we're not being separated for a minute." I was feeling vaguely sick, and used what little energy I had left to fight the sensation down. I tried to smile. "Maybe I have the plague, too."

At that moment the child stopped coughing and opened her eyes. She seemed to be staring through us.

"I'm sorry," she said in a voice that was hardly more than a whisper. "Tell Mummy I'm sorry. I — I didn't — "

Her mouth fell open and a wide vacancy was suddenly frozen on her face. She was dead.

Justine began to cry. She picked the body up and shook it in her arms, as if willing life to return.

"Put her down!" I said sharply. "Put her down and stop that!"

"But — "

"Damn you, we're getting away from here!" I could feel my own hysteria rising. "We're getting out of this bloody mess if we have to crawl on our hands and knees."

It was already too late.

Justine gave me an oddly beseeching look — then suddenly she was sick. She began to retch and shake, and within seconds she couldn't even stand up.

I lay there on the grass watching her helplessly. Every spasm that shook her seemed to be passing through me as well. Like the others, she was changing from a human being into a tormented animal; and even while the thought cut me like a knife I was praying for her to die quickly, praying that she would not suffer long.

I pulled myself towards her and tried to hold her hands, but the strength of the convulsions was too great and I had to let go. The rest of the park became no more than a backcloth to this private tragedy. I was dimly aware of people still being struck down and going through the same terrible stages, of others running about hysterically, but none of it meant anything.

All that mattered was that Justine was dying. It was a fine autumn day, with the sun shining tranquilly through a sky flecked with cotton wool wisps of cloud. But the world below had turned into a nightmare. The thin veil of human dignity had been torn away, and we were as wretched and helpless as a colony of ants poisoned by a gardener of whose existence they were not even aware. I was too weak, too numbed with shock to wonder why or how. All that mattered was that Justine was dying.

As I watched her, time became meaningless. The seconds hung like minutes, the minutes became days, eternity was marked in the lines of pain brought to her face by each racking cough.

There were a few moments when she was lucid, a few even when she could talk.

"Go — go away," she pleaded faintly, and then there was another grating spasm of coughing. "Please . . . please don't stay, darling . . . Don't want you to — to see me . . . like this."

It was no use. I couldn't have moved even if I had wanted to. There was no strength in my limbs. Nothing but terror and grief.

She did not die peacefully as the child had done. She died in the middle of a convulsion, her body slackening suddenly under the strain and falling into an untidy heap like some piece of grotesque sculpture.

I looked at her face, remembering how she used to smile, how her eyes would become almost luminous with pleasure, and love. This other expression that was carved there did not belong to any human being at all.

I had seen too much. Even if I had not still been weak from the operation, I felt I had witnessed more than it is possible to endure while still keeping a grip on one's sanity. The sun was bright but all around me there seemed to be a slowly contracting ring of darkness; and as the darkness closed in, I did not fight against it. I simply prayed that it would become absolute, bringing me the last luxury of total oblivion.

But it was a luxury that I was denied. The unconsciousness lasted for not more than nine or ten hours. The next sensation of which I was aware was a feeling of intense coldness and pain in my operation scar. I opened my eyes and blinked. The sun was low on the horizon and shadows were slanting eerily across the park.

I could hear voices. For one delicious moment, I was convinced that I was just awakening from some fantastic dream and that the world would still be sane and wholesome. But then I saw Justine, and the nightmare was real.

There were still the voices. I sat up too suddenly, and the pain danced through my legs and abdomen until I was afraid I would faint again. But when it had died down, I noticed that there was a jeep not far away. A soldier stood near to it. He seemed to be counting. We saw each other more or less at the same time. The voices I had heard were coming from a radio in the jeep. The soldier switched it off.

I picked myself up and walked unsteadily towards him. He stared at me dumbfounded. "Jesus! You survived it then?"

"Survived what?" I demanded harshly. "I've lived through this bloody mess, if that's what you mean. I wish to God I hadn't."

He meant to be kindly. "You'll feel better in a while, I expect."

"Will I? I watched my wife die."

"Did you, mate?" came the rough answer. "Well, I've got a wife and a couple of kiddies in London, and I don't like to think about them either . . . H-bomb there, about midday."

I gazed dully round the park at the litter of corpses. "How – how did this happen?"

"Sabotage. Happened in about thirty towns. Some bastards must have sprinkled the filthy stuff."

"What stuff?"

He gave me a twisted grin. "Germs. They call the stuff that fixed these poor devils botulinus toxin. They used different bugs in different places."

I looked at him, trying to take the information in. "The war's started, then?"

There was a loud and bitter laugh. "You've been asleep, mate. The war is damn near over. As soon as we knew we were being attacked we threw the lot back at them — 'most every flaming warhead we'd got. Now both sides are packing it in. Shortest war in history. Here, listen to this." He turned to the jeep and switched his radio on.

". . . reports from the radar network indicating that no missiles have been launched by the enemy for almost two hours. It is assumed that the devastation suffered in their home territory is at least comparable with the damage inflicted by them, and the retaliatory use of chemical weapons by our missile groups and air forces, together with pattern bombardment by nuclear weapons, appears to have effectively neutralised their striking power. It is emphasised, however, that further attack by isolated automatic devices may be expected, though these are not anticipated on any wide scale. Meanwhile, although casualties on both sides are estimated to exceed ninety per cent of the civil population, no reliable figures can be given until all available data has been studied. Survivors are assured that centralised military government, together with the means of reorganisation, still exists. A list of survivor-concentration areas, to which all healthy civilians should make their way, will be given at the end of this newscast. Contaminated persons, however, are warned that — "

The soldier switched it off. Suddenly, I saw that his automatic pistol was pointing at my chest. "Must be getting tired with tallying too many stiffs," he apologised. "Got any identification? Orders to check on everybody still alive."

"This is damn silly! Do I look like a saboteur?"

"Who does?" he said indifferently. "Now what about it?"

I saw that his trigger finger had taken the first pressure, and felt hastily in my pockets. "Hospital discharge certificate and driving licence. Will they do?"

"Drop them on the grass and stand back."

He inspected them and seemed satisfied. "Here you are, mate." He handed them back. "What are you going to do now?"

"I haven't given it a bloody thought."

"If I wasn't wearing a uniform," he remarked wistfully, "I know what I'd flaming well do. I'd find myself a nice big car, fill it full of grub and clothes and get the hell out of here."

"Where to?"

"Wide open spaces where there ain't no ruddy people." He waved vaguely at the litter of dead around the park. "When this lot starts cooking, you'll need a gas mask and a flame-thrower. Reckon it'll make the old Plague look like measles in the nursery. Every town's the same. Get out and stay out, that's what I'd do."

I thought about it for a moment or two. "Will you help me bury my wife first? I don't think I can manage it alone."

He gave a grim laugh. "Don't be barmy! Forty-five million dead, more to follow, and you want to bury your wife! Now hop it while the going is good. If any of my lot sees you and they don't shoot, chances are you'll get volunteered into the army. We're a bit short-handed, like."

I gazed at him indecisively for a few moments. Then I turned to go. The logic of events was moving faster than my tired brain could cope with it. Now, I realised, I was living in an age where to survive was considered a suspicious act. In less than a day, civilisation had reverted to barbarism. Those who are not with us are against us . . .

After I had taken a few steps I stopped and called back to him: "What did you say the name of that bug was?"

"Botulinus toxin, mate. Friendly little thing, ain't it? Better thank the Big Boy Upstairs for making you ruddy well immune. But don't press your luck."

I thanked him and made my way out of the park, trying not to look at the bodies I passed.

I didn't know where I was going. I just walked. The streets of the town were also littered with the dead. In the deepening September twilight, their bodies did not look quite so terrible; and at times I pretended to myself that they were just sleeping off the after-effects of one colossal celebration.

A celebration indeed! The coronation of Botulinus Rex!

In the market place among a group of stricken housewives who had presumably been shopping, I saw the body of an old man sprawling in the gutter, still clutching tightly in his hand a long piece of wood to which a torn placard had been pinned.

There was still enough light for me to read its message:

Repent ye, for the Day of Judgment is at hand.

I looked down at the old man and wondered vaguely if he had been surprised at the speed with which his prediction had become stop press news. I wondered, too, if he had expected to find himself included in such a terrible judgment.

Feeling oddly self-conscious, I eased the placard out of his stiff fingers and laid it over the top part of his body — a tattered paper shroud.

Then, feeling like an automaton, I just kept on walking, trying to shut out of my mind the bitter knowledge that there was nowhere to go . . .

The events of the rest of that night are clouded over in my mind. But when dawn came I found that I had been sleeping on one of the benches in a church. There were a million vacant beds in the city to choose from — including one that I knew I could never again sleep in alone — but, somehow, I had been drawn to the church. It was strange, I thought as I sat up and tried to ease the aching in my limbs, because I had never regarded myself as a religious sort of man.

However, I was now no longer alone. Others had evidently been subjected to the same strange motivation. Scattered around the pews there were three or four men, several women — some of them with babies and small children — and, huddled pathetically below the altar, a small boy of about seven who did not seem to belong to anyone present.

It was another bright morning. Sunlight streaming through the tall, narrow windows might almost have convinced us that we were at the beginning of a normal, early autumn day. But as we saw the greyness in each other's faces — the lines of tension and pain and sorrow — we knew with bitter certainty that, no matter how bright the sun, darkness would remain for a long time on the face of the earth . . .

Looking back now over fifty years, when my morning's weaving has been done and my chair has been placed in the farmhouse doorway so that I can gaze across this lovely Derbyshire valley, I hear the voices of the children at play. Children of the Dark Age.

I hear them talking of the Great Ones — the god-like men whose civilisation once spanned continents and whose descendants now live in tribal groups scattered over a strangely quiet world. I hear them talking of the Great Ones, the men of my own generation, the lords of the powered machines, and I realise that it is no longer possible to separate myth from reality. Nor, perhaps, should I try. For children have always needed heroes, just as adults have always needed ideals.

And who knows? It may be that the men who could put satellites into orbit, explore the dark side of the moon, and dream of the conquest of space were truly great. But there is also a dark side to progress. And the greatness of our science provided such engines of destruction that we came near to racial suicide.

Light and darkness, courage and fear, greatness and madness, perpetual conflict of elementals in the enigma of man . . .

Perhaps this Dark Age in which we now live is only transient. Perhaps our racial spirit is such that humanity will inevitably rise again.

But I am now the last of my generation in this valley — the last to remember the Great Ones as they were. I have become, myself, their living epitaph.

The Butterflies

THE SURVEY SHIP *Prometheus* dropped into orbit four hundred miles above the surface of Planet Five. Altogether, there were seven planets in the system. They belonged to the Companion of Sirius, a 'white dwarf' which had the distinction of being the first star to be recognised by terrestrial astronomers before it could be seen.

Planet Five was twenty-two million miles from the mother sun. Sirius itself lay far beyond the confines of the tiny system, being another eighteen hundred million miles away. To the crew of the *Prometheus*, it presented a bright blinding disc, no less impressive than that of its now relatively near Companion. Eventually, the *Prometheus* would voyage closer to the great star to survey her single red planet. But meanwhile, the Companion's system seemed infinitely more attractive — an explorer's paradise.

When the orbit manoeuvre had been successfully completed, the crew of four took themselves to the mess-deck for a celebration. They had something to celebrate, for, so far as they knew, the *Prometheus* was the first ship to navigate satisfactorily under what was called the Relativity Drive — in memory of a very great man and a very imperfect theory.

As soon as they took their places at table, the electronic cooker disgorged roast chicken and a wealth of elegant trimmings, and the refrigerator surrendered a magnum of champagne. Only three of the crew, however, were able to savour the luxury of drinking wine eight and a half light-years away from the vineyard that produced it; for the fourth, a positronic robot, preferred to dine infrequently on a large helping of amperes.

Presently, Captain Trenoy, physicist, astronomer and Master of the *Prometheus*, gave a formal toast; while Whizbang, the robot, watched with red expressionless eyes.

"May our explorations be fruitful," said Captain Trenoy, raising his glass, "may our return be safe, and may the Time Drag not be too heavy on us."

"Amen," said Dr. Blane.

He and Dr. Luiss regarded each other gravely as they lifted their glasses in response. They were both thinking about the same thing. The journey of eight and a half light-years had taken the *Prometheus* eighteen kinetic months, but the ship had left the solar system fifteen earth-years before. By the time it returned, more than thirty-five earth-years would have gone by, though the crew would have aged a mere three and a half years.

Blane, who combined the duties of psychologist, surgeon and physician, was contemplating the spiritual effect of being cut off from one's time and generation. Fortunately or otherwise, it was a problem that would have no reality until the *Prometheus* touched down on earth once more.

Luiss, who held the departments of biochemistry and geology, stared at his champagne and wondered just how long it would take him to go mad.

But such disturbing thoughts slid rapidly into the background as Captain Trenoy, refilling the three glasses, turned the conversation to the immediate problem of touching down on Planet Five. After eighteen months of monotonous starflight, during which there was little to do but make routine checks, routine researches, routine conversation, it was pleasant if unnerving to be faced with the necessity for action.

"Here endeth the first lesson," said the captain, with obscure irony. "And now we'd better fix up some orderly procedure. I am assuming, of course, that you feel we ought to explore as soon as possible." He gazed at his companions enquiringly.

"No reason why we shouldn't," said Dr. Luiss. "I've checked Whizbang's preliminary findings. It doesn't seem as if there will be much difficulty."

"I haven't any objections," agreed Blane. Then he added with a dry smile: "But in view of our experience of the unusual effects of star-sickness, it might be advisable if we sent Whizbang by himself on the first trip."

"I was about to suggest that myself," said Trenoy. "It would be an elementary safety procedure. I think, too, that we should fix it so that we can control the landing rocket from here — just in case Whizbang comes to grief. It would be disastrous if we lost a ferry rocket on the first landing."

"What makes you think I might come to grief Captain?" boomed the robot. "The findings indicate that it's going to be a smooth job."

Trenoy laughed. "You're as logical as they come, Whizbang," he said. "But we poor mortals, lacking your mental equipment, tend to be just a little superstitious. To us, as to the primeval savages, the unknown is always a little magical — in spite of science, in spite of reason and in spite of infallible robots."

Whizbang made strange noises, which his companions had long learned to interpret as robotic laughter.

"So I noticed," he retorted, "when we changed down to Planetary Drive out of R.D. Dr. Blane, our eminent psychologist, was, I recall, furiously stroking a rabbit's paw."

Blane smiled. "No need to feel superior, Whizbang. I saw you playing with a new set of logarithmic notations. It was the first time I've ever seen a robot doodling."

"All right, doodler," said Captain Trenoy. "Tell us what

you've discovered about Planet Five, and we'll decide if there is likely to be any difficulty."

Whizbang recited his information with monotonous efficiency. "Size equates approximately with terrestrial moon. Mass: one over eighty-three point two. Density: three point seven nine. Orbital period: ninety-eight days. Surface: three-fifths solid. Atmosphere: oxygen helium, forty-five fifty. Vegetation: Low type scrub with unusual predominance of blue. No evidence of animal life."

"Suppose we put you down," said Luiss. "What would you do?"

"Take out Radiac and test at ground level," answered Whizbang promptly. "Collect samples and explore to a radius of one hundred yards. Radio verbal report to Captain Trenoy and await instructions."

"Fair enough," said Trenoy. "Down you go."

"I've already checked the ferry rocket," announced Whizbang. "Radiac and sample jars are aboard." He stood up and stretched his nine foot of steel and duralumin. "Shall I make ready, sir?" he asked formally.

"No time like the present," said Trenoy. "Go ahead. Come back and tell us five minutes before point of exit."

The three men stood on the navigation deck of the *Prometheus*, watching the small ferry rocket drift out of the orbit. As it receded in slow motion, Whizbang waved a metal arm cheerily to them from inside his plastiglass dome.

"Are we going to stabilise position over his landing area?" asked Dr. Blane.

"Might as well," said the captain. "There's no reason for playing safe on fuel. Thank God those days are over."

The ferry rocket, gathering negative speed, dropped like a silver bullet to the vast brown and crimson stretch of lava plains below.

"The atmosphere is a piece of cake," said Dr. Luiss happily.

"It looks as if we shall be able to throw off our pressure suits and jump about freely at one-sixth gravity."

"It may be my natural pessimism," observed Dr. Blane, "but I have an odd notion that Planet Five is altogether too obliging. Something tells me that we are in for a few surprises."

"I think you're right," agreed Trenoy. "There always are surprises in this kind of work. It would be somewhat surprising if there weren't." He turned his attention to the two-way radio. "*Prometheus* to Whizbang. *Prometheus* to Whizbang. How are you doing? Over."

He turned a switch, and Whizbang's voice came loud and clear. "Whizbang to Captain Trenoy. I'm skating cautiously through the boundaries of the stratosphere at a hundred thousand feet. Velocity five thousand. Fin temperature fifteen hundred. Internal temperature one hundred and three. It's easy going. Over."

"What does the surface look like?" asked Trenoy.

"As expected, Captain. Blue vegetation areas change shade slightly, purple to crimson. But this may be due to invisible cloud. Over."

"Are you using the auto-pilot? Over," asked the captain. He heard the robot laugh.

"I am more efficient, sir. The auto-pilot would take three minutes longer. Over."

"Watch that fin temperature!" snapped Trenoy. "It's more important than trying to beat the auto-pilot. Over and out."

"Yes, sir. Over and out." Whizbang did his best to sound metallically aggrieved.

Seven minutes later, he touched the ferry rocket down to a perfect landing.

"Whizbang to *Prometheus*. I have touched down on the agreed area on Planet Five. Landing normal. Fuel consumption subnormal. What are your orders? Over."

Back on the *Prometheus*, Captain Trenoy gripped the mike,

glancing at the two men with controlled excitement. He flicked the switch and spoke to Whizbang.

"Do not move. Describe the landscape. Over."

"Sunlight strength four," said Whizbang. "Sky purple to deep blue. Horizon bounded by mountain range. Estimated height of highest peak nine thousand feet. Distance twelve miles. Planetary surface rock; crimson, brown, black. Nearest vegetation three hundred yards away. Pampas type grass, four to six feet high. Colour blue to crimson. Occasional bushes with tendril type leaves, rising to ten feet. Colour, yellow to gold. Animal life: butterfly type, wing-span nine to fifteen inches, multi-coloured, present in large numbers. Estimated cloud of twenty to thirty circling ferry rocket. Large clouds in constant motion above pampas. Over."

On the navigation deck of the survey ship, the atmosphere of excitement intensified.

"Butterflies!" exclaimed Dr. Luiss. "This is going to be interesting. They're quite a reasonably developed evolutionary structure. Obviously there will be other examples of animal life — even if they're only vestigial species relating to the butterflies' development."

Dr. Blane laughed. "Maybe we'll have to take nets with us and dash around like three bug-collecting schoolboys. At one-sixth G, we ought to be able to chase 'em on the wing."

"Not so fast," said Trenoy. "Let's see how they react to Whizbang, and he to them." He flicked the radio switch and spoke once more to the robot, who sat patiently in the pilot's seat of the ferry rocket four hundred miles below.

"*Prometheus* to Whizbang. Take out your Radiac, your atmospherometer and the cine-camera. Make five tests for radioactivity — one general and four specific. Find out the pressure and bulk gases, and bring samples back for lab work. Then take your camera and use fifteen minutes of film. Spread it out — panoramic stuff, telephoto, microphoto and general interest. Also get a butterfly if possible — without harming it. Over."

"Yes, sir," answered Whizbang. "When shall I report? Over."

"Don't be lazy," said Trenoy. "Clip the transceiver on your chest. We'll want a record while you're operating. Over."

"As you say, Captain. Would you like a commentary or question and answer? Over."

"Commentary will do. If I want to ask questions, I'll break in. Over and out."

The men on the navigation deck waited for the robot's monologue to begin. Dr. Luiss went to the manual telescope and began to search the landing area with it. After a moment or two, fancying a shiny dot that he'd picked out was the ferry rocket, he called Captain Trenoy to take a look. Then Whizbang launched into his commentary.

"Transceiver clipped on. I am now descending through oubliette with Radiac. Pressure equalised at nine point nine. Ladder down and entry-port released. I am going down the ladder. General radioactivity normal for oxygen helium at nine point nine. Will now proceed fifty yards from rocket for four radial tests."

Trenoy switched across. "How are the butterflies reacting to your presence?"

"They don't appear to have noticed me yet. Am now making first of radial tests. The butterflies have just begun to notice me. The ones circling above the rocket aren't being tempted, but another cloud of about fifty has risen from the pampas. They're heading straight for me. Now they're circling overhead."

"See if you can get one, but don't alarm them if it can be helped," said Trenoy.

"They're fast on the wing, Captain, and they seem to be able to estimate my range. They're concentrating about twenty feet above my headpiece."

There was a long pause, then: "Flutter by, butterfly! Flutter, flutter, butterfly. Well, well, well! Cut off my coordinators and call me a computer. I think that I shall never see a robot beautiful as me . . ." For the first time in his existence, Whizbang sounded as if he were trying to sing. It was an unmelodious robotic howl. To the men on the *Prometheus* it sounded midway between ecstasy and insanity.

With a startled oath, Captain Trenoy switched in. "Whizbang! What the devil's happening?"

There was no answer for several seconds, then a slurred voice mumbled: "Stell, steel, glorious steel! You'll never know how metallic I feel . . ."

"Whizbang! Answer my question!" Trenoy put every ounce of authority into his command. The response was not encouraging:

"With nuts on his fingers and bolts on his toes, Whizbang needs oiling wherever he goes . . ." The voice trailed away to a crooning whisper. Then silence.

The three men stared at each other in consternation.

"He's off his head," snapped Luiss. "Some damn silly short-circuit has given him D.T.s."

Dr. Blane looked thoughtful. "He was perfectly all right until those butterflies began to concentrate. I wonder . . ."

"What are you thinking of— radiation?" asked Captain Trenoy.

"Something like that," agreed Blane. "It doesn't sound like a mechanical breakdown. I've never heard of a robot getting light-headed because of a short-circuit. It's as if something — some force — had disturbed his equilibrium."

"The ST–EX robots were proofed against every known type of radiation before we left Earth," objected the captain.

"I know," said Blane. "But obviously this is something they weren't proofed against."

"The simple solution is usually correct," said Luiss. "He's

had a breakdown in the language areas. He was all right while he was in the rocket."

"I'll try him again," said Trenoy. He switched over. "Whizbang! Can you hear me? Over."

Silence.

"Whizbang! What's happening? Over."

Silence.

"Whizbang! I order you back to the rocket. Make ready to return to ship! Over."

Still silence.

"Where do we go from here?" asked Captain Trenoy at length. "Any suggestions, gentlemen?"

"Somebody will have to go down in the reserve rocket," said Dr. Luiss. "That somebody had better be me."

"Control your curiosity and be rational," reproved Dr. Blane. "What's the point of hazarding our only other rocket *and* a human being? Have another think."

"Total control!" exclaimed the captain. "The servo-mechanisms for the oubliette and entry-port were synchronised with the auto-pilot before Whizbang went down. Even if we can't get him back to the ferry rocket, we can bring the rocket back here. Then someone might go down and see what's happened to him."

Before Captain Trenoy settled down at the remote control panel, he made a further effort to contact the enigmatic robot, but met with no success. While he was bringing the rocket back to the four hundred mile orbit, Drs. Blane and Luiss developed a quiet and friendly argument concerning the probable cause of Whizbang's failure to respond. Then, as Whizbang still presumably had the transceiver on his chest, Dr. Blane tried to break down his problematic silence by a series of commands, exhortations, trick statements and desperate pleas for help. He met with no result.

"You see," said Luiss triumphantly. "It's a mechanical

breakdown. If he won't even let out a bleat when you tell him it's a matter of life and death, it means only one thing: somewhere the circuit is wrecked."

Dr. Blane still shook his head. "Robots have certain powers of volition," he said slowly. "Weaker, of course, than human volition. Now let us suppose, for the purpose of hypothesis, that something with greater than human volition was able to establish contact with him. Suppose it *willed* him to disobey orders."

"Moonshine," pronounced Dr. Luiss sceptically. "Are you suggesting that Whizbang got himself hypnotised? Because if so, you're getting unnecessarily melodramatic."

"One has to consider possibilities," said Dr. Blane evenly.

"But that's an impossibility! You might just as well consider the possibility of the ground opening up and swallowing him."

"It can't be ruled out," said Blane without humour. "Who are we to assume that the life forms on Planet Five behave conventionally? Those butterflies, for example, might — "

"Might lay duck eggs," grinned Luiss. "Go take a sedative, Doctor. Your imagination is slightly fantastic."

"So very often is the truth," retorted Blane.

While he had been talking, Dr. Blane had watched the progress of the ferry rocket by radar screen and visulator. He saw now that it was within ordinary visual range and, not wishing to prolong a useless discussion, climbed into the astrodome to watch it 'dock' alongside the *Prometheus*.

"I still think one man only should go, and that he should not leave the rocket — unless, of course, he finds a reasonable explanation for Whizbang's silence." Watching the captain closely, Dr. Blane could see, even before he replied, that Trenoy was unconvinced.

"Perhaps you are letting superstition take precedence over scientific caution," said Captain Trenoy, with the faintest of smiles. "I think our arrangements will be quite adequate. We shall take u/s vibrators and H.F.C. beam apparatus. Unless there is an emergency, one of us will remain in the rocket all the time."

"You may encounter something against which the vibrators and H.F.C. weapon will be useless."

"In that case, it certainly won't be physical," observed Dr. Luiss with irony.

"Exactly," said Blane. He wanted to add something else, but couldn't find the right words.

"We'd better get moving," remarked Trenoy. "We may have a small search on our hands before we find Whizbang."

Dr. Blane accepted defeat gracefully. "Good hunting," he said. "I'll be glued to the transceiver."

"We'll bring you back a couple of tame butterflies to play with," promised Luiss gaily, as he fixed the headpiece on his pressure suit.

When they had checked their pressure and personal radios, the two men left the navigation deck and made their way to the starboard airlock and entry-port. From the astrodome, Dr. Blane watched the small ferry rocket fall out of the orbit as it gathered negative speed. Twenty minutes later, he heard Luiss's voice telling him that they had touched down safely at the landing area.

"We can see Whizbang," said Luiss excitedly. "He's about a couple of hundred yards away, balancing on one foot like a heavyweight ballerina. The butterflies are still circling over him." He chuckled. "Bet they're thinking that, if he's a specimen of alien culture, they did well to remain butterflies. He looks, though, almost as if he belongs to the landscape."

"Any other signs of life — apart from the butterflies?" asked Dr. Blane.

"No, not yet. I'm going out to have a look at our petrified robot, so I'll hand over to Captain Trenoy."

Dr. Blane's hands were trembling, his face was white. He paced the navigation deck rapidly, casting suspicious glance now and again at the nine-foot robot, who stood waiting patiently.

"Tell me your story again," he commanded. "We will consider the inaccuracy in relation to the whole." It was no good calling the robot a liar, because Whizbang was mechanically incapable of lying. He was, however, quite capable of being inaccurate.

Responding to the order, he again related his story in a voice which faltered only very slightly when he came to the part which Dr. Blane was able to disprove.

"The first thing I remember, sir," said Whizbang, "was Dr. Luiss bawling at me for being what he called a broken-down cretin. Previous to that, my only recollection is of reporting back to ship as I began the first radial test and the butterflies came."

"Where were the butterflies when Dr. Luiss spoke to you?"

"They were circling the rocket again, sir, but there were none near me or Dr. Luiss. The clouds skimming over the pampas seemed bigger than before, but that was probably because Dr. Luiss had disturbed them. He told me he'd given the group circling above my head half a second of ultrasonic vibration, and that it had scared them away."

"Did he tell you his further intentions?"

"He said he was going to look around within a hundred yards radius, and collect samples. Then he ordered me back to the rocket."

"What did Captain Trenoy do?"

"He questioned me and then spoke to you, sir, describing the landscape in detail and giving you a commentary on Dr. Luiss's activities."

"Why did Captain Trenoy leave the rocket?"

"Dr. Luiss called to him over the personal wavelength in a very excited voice. He said that he'd found the skeleton of a large quadruped with a cranial capacity of approximately one cubic foot. He said that the animals on Planet Five must have reached a very high evolutionary stage. Finally, he suggested that Captain Trenoy came and had a look for himself, leaving me in the rocket. The Captain said it didn't seem a very intelligent procedure, but Dr. Luiss replied that there were no living animals in sight, that the pampas was far enough away to give a reasonable safety margin, and that if the butterflies came near they could certainly be dispersed by ultrasonics."

Dr. Blane nodded. "That's true. I heard snatches of their conversation over the transceiver. Did Captain Trenoy give you any instructions before he left?"

"He put me through a simple test to make sure that my memory and reasoning ability were not damaged. Then he told me to stay in the rocket and not leave it under any circumstances."

"At which point," said Dr. Blane thoughtfully, "you took over the commentary."

"That is so," agreed Whizbang, with a trace of hesitation. "I continued with the commentary until you gave me instructions to return to the *Prometheus*."

"But since I did not radio those instructions," said Blane, staring hard at the robot, "we are left with two possibilities. Name them!"

The robot was silent for a moment. Then he spoke slowly. "One: that my circuits are damaged. Two: that some other entity caused me to receive the message."

"Which do you think it is?" snapped Blane.

"If you would like to test me, sir . . ." began Whizbang.

"To hell with tests! Which is it?"

"I think my circuits are intact."

"Then you think the message originated elsewhere?"

"Yes, sir — if you are sure you did not send it."

Blane controlled himself with difficulty. "We'll leave that

for the moment. Repeat verbatim your commentary to the point where I apparently ordered you to return."

"Whizbang to *Prometheus*," said the robot. "Captain Trenoy is now descending through the oubliette to join Dr. Luiss. Dr. Luiss is examining the skeleton of the quadruped. The nearest butterflies are about two hundred yards away. There is a small cloud of them rising from the pampas. They appear to be circling aimlessly at an altitude of a hundred and fifty feet. Captain Trenoy has now joined Dr. Luiss. They are digging together by the side of the skeleton. The butterflies are drifting slightly. Captain Trenoy glances at them every few seconds, while continuing his work. Now the cloud is almost above the skeleton at about two hundred feet. Suddenly the two men stand up. They stare at the butterflies. Dr. Luiss remarks over his personal radio that it is the most incredible thing he ever heard. Suddenly the butterflies drop fifty feet. At the same time, Captain Trenoy and Dr. Luiss begin to unscrew their headpieces very slowly . . ." Whizbang stopped.

"Go on! Go on!" urged Dr. Blane.

"Then, sir," said Whizbang, "I heard your voice through the transceiver. You said: '*Prometheus* to Whizbang, return to orbit immediately. Urgent! Return to orbit immediately. Over and out.' "

"What happened next?" asked Blane.

"I informed Captain Trenoy over the ground radio. He said: 'You must obey, Whizbang. You must always obey.' So I sealed the rocket and took off as rapidly as possible. By the time I had equalised gravity, and was beginning to release power, the butterflies had dropped another fifty feet. Captain Trenoy and Dr. Luiss were standing motionless. They had taken off their headpieces. Then I had to let in power, and the rocket climbed."

"Was Captain Trenoy's voice normal?"

"No, sir. He spoke slowly and very quietly."

"Are you sure it was his voice?"

"Yes, sir."

For two or three minutes, Dr. Blane strode nervously up and down, tortured by indecision. Finally, he made up his mind.

"I am going down, Whizbang."

"Yes, sir."

"You will remain on duty here."

Dr. Blane set the rocket down gently. He unstrapped himself, stood up, and gazed through the plastiglass dome. A quarter of a mile away, he saw two motionless figures standing erect on a stretch of brown and crimson rock. Focusing the binoculars, Dr. Blane made out a cloud of butterflies hovering about ten feet above the men. The heads of his two companions were strangely obscured, but dull sunlight glinted on the surface of a headpiece lying at the feet of one of them.

Grimly, Dr. Blane reached for the two u/s vibrators. Placing them carefully in the pockets of his pressure suit, he descended through the oubliette. A few seconds later, he stood on the strange surface of Planet Five.

Gripping a vibrator in each hand, he looked cautiously around him, and then up at the sky. Apart from the cloud above the two men a quarter of a mile away, and the endless activity on the pampas, there did not seem to be any immediate danger.

Slowly Dr. Blane walked towards his companions. At one hundred yards he stopped, stood quite still, took careful aim. He gave the cloud of butterflies a two-second dose of vibration. They scattered with much violent flapping, and a few dropped crazily down to the rocky surface. As they fell, another small cloud rose, and Dr. Blane knew then what had been obscuring the heads of Trenoy and Luiss. He fought back a sharp involuntary sickness and marched on.

At fifty yards, he thought it was an illusion; but at twenty-five yards it became inescapable fact. Dr. Blane was approaching two men in pressure suits who were dead but still standing. Their clean-picked skulls were fixed in two barren grins.

In his own pressure suits Blane was sweating with panic. A sixth sense warned him to turn round and run. But it was already too late. For, to Dr. Blane's heightened perception, there came the first faint strains of a vast compelling music. It was the pattern, the experience, the mobility, the sheer harmony of a thousand symphonies condensed into a single chord.

Turning, with a tremendous effort, he saw the butterflies rising from the pampas, and knew — in the instant before that colossal theme of ecstasy blocked all thought — that presently the butterflies would begin to circle lower and lower.

There were tears in Dr. Blane's eyes. But they were not tears for his own approaching death. They were the only way in which he, and his companions before him, could react to an experience that was profound beyond any known to man; that was compelling and final, tearing its way past the flimsy threshold of human consciousness.

The vibrators dropped from his impatient fingers. Slowly, hypnotically, Dr. Blane fumbled for the release clips of his headpiece. And the music swelled like sacramental thunder, the soundless music of thousands of multi-coloured butterflies, thousands of insect carnivores closing in upon their selected prey. And across the pampas, across the brown and crimson rocks, myriads of flapping wings proclaimed their centralisation of power — submergence of the individual in a tremendous group identity.

Dr. Blane stood there, unable to think, unable to see, unable to move — waiting for the butterflies to descend. Waiting for the crunch of small but powerful mandibles . . .

The short nine-hour day on Planet Five drew quietly to a close. Then the sun, known to earthlings as the Companion of Sirius, began to slip smoothly over a blue and purple horizon. Presently, the butterflies rose, winging across the pampas to their nocturnal bat-like roosts. Presently, there was only the solitude of night, the remote mystery of stars . . .

The survey ship *Prometheus* remained in orbit for ten more days. Whizbang, the robot, kept a steady vigil by the transceiver on the navigation deck, in accordance with instructions. But the lack of response to his repeated signals forced him to the obvious conclusion.

He satisfied himself that there was one very sound reason why there could be no survivors; for men, unlike robots, cannot exist without water. Unfortunately, the water on Planet Five was different from its terrestrial counterpart, belonging to a different geological cycle. Its chemical symbol was infinitely more complex than a mere H_2O.

So Whizbang brought in an open verdict, secure in the conviction that his masters could no longer be alive.

He had, however, no knowledge of the manner of their deaths. When he, too, had been a victim of the butterfly-mind, he had not heard the compelling music, for it was reaching to something far deeper than a synthetic brain. He had merely been positronically disturbed. He had merely been, for the first time in his robotic existence, asleep while his batteries were still powered. Nor could he know that, with a superior act of volition, the butterfly-mind had simply willed him to go away. Being metallic, he was not a possible source of food; and not being a source of food, he was only irrelevant.

But even a robot must rationalise when forced to act without human command. So Whizbang had found it necessary to 'invent' Dr. Blane's instruction to return to the *Prometheus*.

Standing now on the navigation deck, he stared with

red expressionless eyes at the surface of Planet Five.

At last, he reached a decision. The information would have to be given to other human beings, who would then assume responsibility.

Whizbang jerked himself up into the astrodome and began to take bearings. As he worked, he knew neither happiness nor anxiety, neither hope nor despair, neither regret nor relief.

He knew only that he could handle the Relativity Drive more efficiently than men.

EDMUND COOPER

SEA-HORSE IN THE SKY

At first he thought it was all part of some crazy nightmare. But it wasn't.

Russell Grahame, M.P. was only one of a handful of passengers flying from Stockholm to London. One moment flying peacefully in the sky, the next lying in an un-Earthly green coffin.

Grahame was the first to emerge from this strange resting place. But for him, as well as for the others, it had been only the first ecliptical experience. Soon all were to find themselves lost in a bizarre world of Mediaeval knights. Stone Age warriors, and gremlins, caught unalterably in the weirdest cocoon of Time.

CORONET BOOKS

JACK VANCE

MARUNE: ALASTOR 993

Man With No Past

From his fabulous palace on Numenes, the Connatic ruled the sprawling Alastor Clustor . . . and kept track of the doings of each of his trillion or more subjects. But there was one man he knew nothing about—for the past life of the wanderer called Pardero was a complete mystery.

Pardero set himself two goals. To find out who he was . . . and to find his enemy, the person who had stolen his memory.

Psychologists deduced that his home world must be the mysterious Marune . . . a planet lit by four shifting suns, Pardero made his way there—and was hailed as the Kaiark Efraim, ruler of the shadowed realm.

Uncovering his lost identity had been comparatively simple. Finding his sworn enemy would be more difficult. . . there were so many people to choose from!

CORONET BOOKS

KARL EDWARD WAGNER

NIGHT WINDS

KANE

The Mystic Swordsman ranges Earth and Time to confront the demons of darkness

Where once the mighty Kane has passed, no one who lives forgets. Now, down the trail of past battles, Kane travels again. To the ruins of a devastated city peopled only with half-men and the waif they call their queen. To the half-burnt tavern where a woman Kane wronged long ago holds his child in keeping for the Devil. To the cave kingdom of the giants where glory and its aftermath await discovery. To the house of death itself where Kane retrieves a woman to love.

The past, the future, the present—all are one for Kane as he travels through the centuries.

CORONET BOOKS